A Cumberland Vendetta

John Fox, Jr.

Contents

A CUMBERLAND VENDETTA

BY

John Fox, Jr.

I

THE cave had been their hiding-place as children; it was a secret refuge now against hunger or darkness when they were hunting in the woods. The primitive meal was finished; ashes were raked over the red coals; the slice of bacon and the little bag of meal were hung high against the rock wall; and the two stepped from the cavern into a thicket of rhododendrons.

Parting the bushes toward the dim light, they stood on a massive shoulder of the mountain, the river girding it far below, and the afternoon shadows at their feet. Both carried guns-the tall mountaineer, a Winchester; the boy, a squirrel rifle longer than himself. Climbing about the rocky spur, they kept the same level over log and bowlder and through bushy ravine to the north. In half an hour, they ran into a path that led up home from the river, and they stopped to rest on a cliff that sank in a solid black wall straight under them. The sharp edge of a steep corn-field ran near, and, stripped of blade and tassel, the stalks and hooded ears looked in the coming dusk a little like monks at prayer. In the sunlight across the river the corn stood thin and frail. Over there a drought was on it; and when drifting thistle-plumes marked the noontide of the year, each yellow stalk had withered blades and an empty sheath. Every-where a look of vague trouble lay upon the face of the mountains, and when the wind blew, the silver of the leaves showed ashen. Autumn was at hand.

There was no physical sign of kinship between the two, half-brothers though they were. The tall one was dark; the boy, a foundling, had flaxen hair, and was stunted and ˜lender. He was a dreamy˜looking little fellow, and one may easily find his like throughout the Cumberland -paler than his fellows, from staying much indoors, with half-haunted face, and eyes that are deeply pathetic when not cunning; ignorantly credited with idiocy and uncanny powers; treated with much forbearance, some awe, and a little contempt; and suffered to do his pleasure-nothing, or much that is strange-without comment.

"I tell ye, Rome," he said, taking up the thread of talk that was broken at the cave, "when Uncle Gabe says he's afeard thar's trouble comm', hit's a-comm'; 'n' I want you to git me a Winchester. I'm a-gittin' big enough now. I kin shoot might' nigh as good as you, 'n' whut am I fit fer with this hyeh old pawpaw pop-gun?"

"I don't want you fightin', boy, I've told ye. Y'u air too little 'n' puny, 'n' I want ye to stay home 'n' take keer o' mam 'n' the cattle-ef fightin' does come, I reckon thar won't be triuch."

Don't ye? " cried the boy, with sharp contempt-" with ole Jas Lewallen a-devilin' Uncle Rufe, 'n' that blackheaded young Jas a-climbin' on stumps over thar 'cross the river, n' crowin' n' sayin' out open in Hazlan that ye air afeard o him? Yes; 'n' he called me a idgit." The boy's voice broke into a whimper of rage.

"Shet up, Isom! Don't you go gittin' mad now. You'll be sick ag'in. I'll tend to him when the time comes." Rome spoke with rough kindness, but ugly lines had gathered at his mouth and forehead. The boy's tears came and went easily. He drew his sleeve across his eyes, and looked up the river. Beyond the bend, three huge birds rose into the sunlight and floated toward them. Close at hand, they swerved side-wise.

"They hain't buzzards," he said, standing up, his anger gone; "look at them straight wings!

Again the eagles swerved, and two shot across the river. The third dropped with shut wings to the bare crest of a gaunt old poplar under them.

"Hit's a young un, Rome Y" said the boy, excitedly. "He's goin' to wait thar tell the old uns come back. Gimme that gun!

Catching up the Winchester, he slipped over the ledge; and Rome leaned suddenly forward, looking down at the river.

A group of horsemen had ridden around the bend, and were coming at a walk down the other shore. Every man carried something across his saddle-bow. There was a gray horse among them - young Jasper's - and an evil shadow came into Rome's face, and quickly passed. Near a strip of woods the gray turned up the mountain from the party, and on its back he saw the red glint of a woman's dress. With a half-smile he watched the scarlet figure ride from the woods, and climb slowly up through the sunny corn. On the spur above and full in the rich yellow light, she halted, half turning in her saddle. He rose to his feet, to his full height, his head bare, and thrown far back between his big shoulders, and, still as statues, the man and the woman looked at each other across the gulf of darkening air. A full minute the woman sat motionless, then rode on. At the edge of the woods she stopped and turned again.

The eagle under Rome leaped one stroke in the air, and dropped like a clod into the sea of leaves. The report of the gun and a faint cry of triumph rose from below. It was good marksmanship, but on the cliff Rome did not heed it. Something had fluttered in the air above the girl's head, and he laughed aloud. She was waving her bonnet at him.

II

JUST where young Stetson stood, the mountains racing along each bank of the Cumberland had sent out against each other, by mutual impulse, two great spurs. At the river's brink they stopped sheer, with crests uplifted, as though some hand at the last moment had hurled them apart, and had led the water through the breach to keep them at peace. To-day the crags looked seamed by thwarted passion; and, sullen with firs, they made fit symbols of the human hate about the base of each.

When the feud began, no one knew. Even the original cause was forgotten. Both families had come as friends from Virginia long ago, and had lived as enemies nearly half a century. There was hostility before the war, but, until then, little bloodshed. Through the hatred of change, characteristic of the mountaineer the world over, the Lewallens were for the Union. The Stetsons owned a few slaves, and they fought for them. Peace found both still neighbors and worse foes. The war armed them, and brought back an ancestral contempt for human life; it left them a heritage of lawlessness that for mutual protection made necessary the very means used by their feudal forefathers; personal hatred supplanted its dead issues, and with them the war went on. The Stetsons had a good strain of Anglo-Saxon blood, and owned valley-lands; the Lewallens kept store and made "moonshine"; so kindred and debtors and kindred and tenants were arrayed with one or the other leader, and gradually the retainers of both settled on one or the other side of the river. In time of hostility the Cumberland came to be the boundary between life and death for the dwellers on each shore. It was feudalism born again.

Above one of the spurs each family had its home; the Stetsons, under the seared face of Thunderstruck Knob; the Lewallens, just beneath the wooded rim of Wolf's Head. The eaves and chimney of each cabin were faintly visible from the porch of the other. The first light touched the house of the Stetsons; the last, the Lewallen cabin. So there were times when the one could not turn to the sunrise nor the other to the sunset but with a curse in his heart, for his eye must fall on the home of his enemy.

For years there had been peace. The death of Rome Stetson's father from ambush, and the fight in the court-house square, had forced it. After that fight only four were left-old Jasper Lewallen and young Jasper, the boy Rome and his uncle, Rufe Stetson. Then Rufe fled to the West, and the Stetsons were helpless. For three years no word was heard of him, but the hatred burned in the heart of Rome's mother, and was traced deep in her grim old face while she patiently waited the day of retribution. It smouldered, too, in the hearts of the women of both clans who had lost husbands or sons or lovers; and the friends and kin of each had little to do with one another, and met and passed with watchful eyes. Indeed, it would take so little to turn peace to war that the wonder was that peace had lived so long. Now trouble was at hand. Rufe Stetson had come back at last, a few months since, and had quietly opened store at the county-seat, Hazlan-a little town five miles up the river, where Troubled Fork runs seething into the Cumberland-a point of neutrality for the factions, and consequently a battIe-ground. Old Jasper's store was at the other end of the town, and the old man had never been known to brook competition. He had driven three men from Hazlan during the last term of peace for this offence, and everybody knew that the fourth must leave or fight. Already Rufe Stetson had been warned not to appear outside his door after dusk. Once or twice his wife had seen skulking shadows under the trees across the road, and a tremor of anticipation ran along both banks of the Cumberland.

III

A FORTNIGHT later, court came. Rome was going to Hazlan, and the feeble old Stetson mother limped across the porch from the kitchen, trailing a Winchester behind her. Usually he went unarmed, but he took the gun now, as she gave it, in silence.

The boy Isom was not well, and Rome had told him to ride the horse. But the lad had gone on afoot to his duties at old Gabe Bunch's mill, and Rome himself rode down Thunderstruck Knob through the mist and dew of the early morning. The sun was coming up over Virginia, and through a dip in Black Mountain the foothills beyond washed in blue waves against its white disk. A little way down the mountain, the rays shot through the gap upon him, and, lancing the mist into tatters, and lighting the dew-drops, set the birds singing. Rome rode, heedless of it all, under primeval oak and poplar, and along rain-clear brooks and happy waterfalls, shut in by laurel and rhododendron, and singing past mossy stones and lacelike ferns that brushed his stirrup. On the brow of every cliff he would stop to look over the trees and the river to the other shore, where the gray line of a path ran aslant Wolf's Head, and was lost in woods above and below.

At the river he rode up-stream, looking still across it. Old Gabe Bunch halloed to him from the doorway of the mill, as he splashed through the creek, and Isom's thin face peered through a breach in the logs. At the ford beyond, he checked his horse with a short oath of pleased surprise. Across the water, a scarlet dress was moving slowly past a brown field of corn. The figure was bonneted, but he knew the girl's walk and the poise of her head that far away. Just who she was, however, he did not know, and he sat irresolute. He had seen her first a month since, paddling along the other shore, erect, and with bonnet off and hair down; she had taken the Lewallen path up the mountain. Afterward, he saw her going at a gallop on young Jasper's gray horse, bareheaded again, and with her hair loose to the wind, and he knew she was one of his enemies. He thought her the girl people said young Jasper was going to marry, and he had watched her the more closely. From the canoe she seemed never to notice him; but he guessed, from the quickened sweep of her paddle, that she knew he was looking at her, and once, when he halted on his way home up the mountain, she half turned in her saddle and looked across at him. This happened again, and then she waved her bonnet at him. It was bad enough, any Stetson seeking any Lewallen for a wife, and for him to court young Jasper's sweetheart-it was a thought to laugh at. But the mischief was done. The gesture thrilled him, whether it meant defiance or good-will, and the mere deviltry of such a courtship made him long for it at every sight of her with the river between them. At once he began to plan how he should get near her, but, through some freak, she had paid no further heed to him. He saw her less often-for a week, in-deed, he had not seen her at all till this day-and the forces that hindrance generates in an imperious nature had been at work within him. The chance now was one of gold, and with his life in his hand he turned into the stream. Across, he could see something white on her shoulder-an empty bag. It was grinding~day, and she was going to the mill-the Lewallen mill. She stopped as he galloped up, and turned, pushing back her bonnet with one hand; and he drew rein. But the friendly, expectant light in her face kindled to such a blaze of anger in her eyes that he struck his horse violently, as though the beast had stopped of its own accord, and, cursing himself, kept on. A little farther, he halted again. Three horsemen, armed with Winchesters, were jogging along toward town ahead of him, and he wheeled about sharply. The girl, climbing rapidly toward Steve Bray-ton's cabin, was out of the way, but he was too late to reach the ford again. Down the road two more Lewallens with guns were in sight, and he lashed his horse into the stream where the water was deep. Old Gabe, looking from the door of his mill, quit laughing to himself; and under cover of the woods, the girl watched man and horse fighting the tide. Twice young Stetson turned his head. But his enemies apparently had not seen him, and horse and rider scrambled up the steep bank and under shelter of the trees. The girl had evidently learned who he was. Her sudden anger was significant, as was the sight of the Lewallens going armed to court, and Rome rode on, uneasy.

When he reached Troubled Fork, in sight of Hazlan, he threw a cartridge into place and shifted the slide to see that it was ready for use. Passing old Jasper's store on the edge of the town, he saw the old man's bushy head through the open door, and Lewallens and Braytons crowded out on the steps and looked after him. All were armed. Twenty paces farther he met young Jasper on his gray, and the look on his enemy's face made him grip his rifle. With a flashing cross-fire from eye to eye, the two passed, each with his thumb on the hammer of his Winchester. The groups on the court-house steps stopped talking as he rode by, and turned to look at him. He saw none of his own friends, and he went on at a gallop to Rufe Stetson's store. His uncle was not in sight. Steve Marcum and old Sam Day stood in the porch, and inside a woman was crying. Several Stetsons were near, and all with grave faces gathered about him.

He knew what the matter was before Steve spoke. His uncle had been driven from town. A last warning had come to him on the day before. The hand of a friend was in the caution, and Rufe rode away at dusk. That night his house was searched by men masked and armed. The Lewallens were in town, and were ready to fight. The crisis had come.

IV

BACK at the mill old Gabe was troubled. Usually he sat in a cane-bottomed chair near the hopper, whittling, while the lad tended the mill, and took pay in an oaken toll-dish smooth with the use of half a century. But the incident across the river that morning had made the old man uneasy, and he moved restlessly from his chair to the door, and back again, while the boy watched him, wondering what the matter was, but asking no questions. At noon an old mountaineer rode by, and the miller hailed him.

"Any news in town?" he asked.

"Hain't been to town. Reckon fightin' 's goin' on thar from whut I heerd." The careless, high-pitched answer brought the boy with wide eyes to the door.

Whut d'ye hear? " asked Gabe. Jes heerd fightin' 's goin' on!

Then every man who came for his meal brought a wild rumor from town, and the old miller moved his chair to the door, and sat there whittling fast, and looking anxiously toward Hazlan. The boy was in a fever of unrest, and old Gabe could hardly keep him in the mill. In the middle of the afternoon the report of a rifle came down the river, breaking into echoes against the cliffs below, and Isom ran out the door, and stood listening for another, with an odd contradiction of fear and delight on his eager face. In a few moments Rome Stetson galloped into sight, and, with a shrill cry of relief, the boy ran down the road to meet him, and ran back, holding by a stirrup. Young Stetson's face was black with passion, and his eyes were heavy with drink. At the door of the mill he swung from his horse, and for a moment was hardly able to speak from rage. There had been no fight. The Stetsons were few and unprepared. They had neither the guns nor, without Rufe, the means to open the war, and they believed Rufe had gone for arms. So they had chafed in the store all day, and all day Lewallens on horseback and on foot were in sight; and each was a taunt to every Stetson, and, few as they were, the young and hot-headed wanted to go out and fight. In the afternoon a tale-bearer had brought some of Jasper's boasts to Rome, and, made reckless by moonshine and much brooding, he sprang up to lead them. Steve Marcum, too, caught up his gun, but old Sam's counsel checked him, and the two by force held Rome back. A little later the Lewallens left town. The Stetsons, too, disbanded, and on the way home a last drop of gall ran Rome's cup of bitterness over. Opposite Steve Brayton's cabin a jet of smoke puffed from the bushes across the river, and a bullet furrowed the road in front of him. That was the shot they had heard at the mill. Somebody was drawing a dead-line," and Rome wheeled his horse at the brink of it. A mocking yell came over the river, and a gray horse flashed past an open space in the bushes. Rome knew the horse and knew the yell; young Jasper was "bantering" him. Nothing maddens the mountaineer like this childish method of insult; and telling of it, Rome sat in a corner, and loosed a torrent of curses against young Lewallen and his clan.

Old Gabe had listened without a word, and the strain in his face was eased. Always the old man had stood for peace. He believed it had come after the court-house fight, and he had hoped against hope, even when Rufe came back to trade against old Jasper; for Rufe was big and good-natured, and unsuspected of resolute purpose, and the Lewallens' power had weakened. So, now that Rufe was gone again, the old miller half believed he was gone for good. Nobody was hurt; there was a chance yet for peace, and with a rebuke on his tongue and relief in his face, the old man sat back in his chair and went on whittling. The boy turned eagerly to a crevice in the logs and, trembling with excitement, searched the other bank for Jasper's gray horse, going home.

He called me a idgit," he said to himself, with a threatening shake of his head. "Jes wouldn't I like to hev a chance at him! Rome ull git him! Rome ull git him!"

There was no moving point of white on the broad face of the mountains nor along the river road. Jasper was yet to come and, with ears alert to every word behind him, the lad fixed his eyes where he should see him first.

"Oh, he didn't mean to hit me. Not that he ain't mean enough to shoot from the bresh," Rome broke out savagely. "That's jes whut I'm afeard he will do. Thar was too much daylight fer him. Ef he jes don't come a-sneakin' over hyeh, 'n' waitin' in the lorrel atter dark fer me, it's all I axe."

Waitin' in the lorrel! " Old Gabe could hold back no longer. "Hit's a shame, a burn-in' shame! I don' know whut things air comm' to! 'Pears like all you young folks think about is killin' somebody. Folks usen to talk about how fer they could kill a deer; now it's how fer they kin kill a man. I hev knowed the time when a man would 'a' been druv out o' the county fer drawin' a knife ur a pistol; 'n' ef a feller was ever killed, it was kinder accidental, by a Barlow. I reckon folks got use' to weepons 'n' killin' 'n' bushwhackin' in the war. Looks like it's been gittin' wuss ever sence, 'n' now hit's dirk 'n' Winchester, 'n' shootin' from the bushes all the time. Hit's wuss 'n stealin' money to take a feller-creetur' s life that way!

The old miller's indignation sprang from memories of a better youth. For the courtesies of the code went on to the Blue Grass, and before the war the mountaineer fought with English fairness and his fists. It was a disgrace to use a deadly weapon in those days; it was a disgrace now not to use it.

Oh, I know all the excuses folks make," he went on: " hit's fa'r fer one as 'tis fer t'other; y'u can't fight a man fa'r 'n' squar' who'll shoot you in the back; a pore man can't fight money in the couhts; 'n' thar hain't no witnesses in the lorrel but leaves; 'n' dead men don't hev much to say. I know it all. Hit's cur'us, but it act'-ally looks like lots o' decent young folks hev got usen to the idee-thar's so much of it goin' on, 'n' thar's so much talk 'bout killin' 'n' layin' out in the lorrel. Reckon folks 'll git to pesterm' women n' strangers bimeby, 'n' robbin' 'n' thievin'. Hit's bad enough thar's so leetle law thet folks hev to take it in their own hands oncet in a while, but this shootin' from the bresh-hit's p'int'ly a sin 'n' shame! Why," he concluded, pointing his remonstrance as he always did, "I seed your grandad and young Jas's fight up thar in Hazlan full two hours 'fore the war-fist and skull-'n' your grandad was whooped. They got up and shuk hands. I don't see why folks can't fight that way now. I wish Rufe 'n' old Jas 'n' you 'n' young Jas could have it out fist and skull, 'n' stop this killin' o' people like hogs. Thar's nobody left but you four. But thar's no chance o' that, I reckon."

"I'll fight him anyway, 'n' I reckon ef he don't die till I lay out in the lorrel fer him, he'll live a long time. Ef a Stetson ever done sech meanness as that I never heerd it."

Nother hev I," said the old man, with quick justice. " You air a over-bearin' race, all o' ye, but I never knowed ye to be that mean. Hit's all the wus fer ye thet ye air in sech doin's. I tell ye, Rome—

A faint cry rose above the drone of the millstones, and old Gabe stopped with open lips to listen. The boy's face was pressed close to the logs. A wet paddle had flashed into the sunlight from out the bushes across the river. He could just see a canoe in the shadows under them, and with quick suspicion his brain pictured Jasper's horse hitched in the bushes, and Jasper stealing across the river to waylay Rome. But the canoe moved slowly out of sight downstream and toward the deep water, the paddler unseen, and the boy looked around with a weak smile. Neither seemed to have heard him. Rome was brooding, with his sullen face in his hands; the old miller was busy with his own thoughts; and the boy turned again to his watch.

Jasper did not come. Isom's eyes began to ache from the steady gaze, and now and then he would drop them to the water swirling beneath. A slow wind swayed the overhanging branches at the mouth of the stream, and under them was an eddy. Escaping this, the froth and bubbles raced out to the gleams beating the air from the sunlit river. He saw one tiny fleet caught; a mass of yellow scum bore down and, sweeping through bubbles and eddy, was itself struck into fragments by something afloat. A tremulous shadow shot through a space of sunlight into the gloom cast by a thicket of rhododendrons, and the boy caught his breath sharply. A moment more, and the shape of a boat and a human figure quivered on the water running under him. The stern of a Lewallen canoe swung into the basin, and he sprang to his feet.

"Rome!" The cry cut sharply through the drowsy air. " Thar he is! Hit's Jas"

The old miller rose to his feet. The boy threw himself behind the sacks of grain. Rome wheeled for his rifle, and stood rigid before the door. There was a light step without, the click of a gun-lock within; a shadow fell across the doorway, and a girl stood at the threshold with an empty bag in her hand.

V

WITH a little cry she shrank back a step. Her face paled and her lips trembled, and for a moment she could not speak. But her eyes swept the group, and were fixed in two points of fire on Rome.

"Why don't ye shoot! "she asked, scornfully.

"I hev heerd that the Stetsons have got to makin war on women-folks, but I never believed it afore." Then she turned to the miller.

Kin I git some more meal hyeh? " she asked. " Or have ye stopped sellin' to folks on t'other side? " she added, in a tone that sought no favor.

"You kin have all ye want," said old Gabe, quietly.

"The mill on Dead Crick is broke ag'in," she continued, " 'n' co'n is skeerce on our side. We'll have to begin buyin' purty soon, so I thought I'd save totin' the co'n down hyeh." She handed old Gabe the empty bag.

Well," said he, " as it air gittin' late, 'n' ye have to climb the mountain ag'in, I'll let ye have that comm' out o' the hopper now. Take a cheer."

The girl sat down in the low chair, and, loos ening the strings of her bonnet, pushed it back from her head. An old-fashioned horn comb dropped to the floor, and when she stooped to pick it up she let her hair fall in a head about her shoulders. Thrusting one hand under it, she calmly tossed the whole mass of chestnut and gold over the back of the chair, where it fell rippling like water through a bar of sunlight. With head thrown back and throat bared, she shook it from side to side, and, slowly coiling it, pierced it with the coarse comb. Then passing her hands across her forehead and temples, as women do, she folded them in her lap, and sat motionless. The boy, crouched near, held upon her the mesmeric look of a serpent. Old Gabe was peering covertly from under the brim of his hat, with a chuckle at his lips. Rome had fallen back to a corner of the mill, sobered, speechless, his rifle in a nerveless hand. The passion that fired him at the boy's warning had as swiftly gone down at sight of the girl, and her cutting rebuke made him hot again with shame. He was angry, too-more than angry-because he felt so helpless, a sensation that was new and stifling. The scorn of her face, as he remembered it that morning, hurt him again while he looked at her. A spirit of contempt was still in her eyes, and quivering about her thin lips and nostrils. She had put him beneath further notice, and yet every toss of her head, every movement of her hands, seemed meant for him, to irritate him. And once, while she combed her hair, his brain whirled with an impulse to catch the shining stuff in one hand and to pinion both her wrists with the other, Just to show her that he was master, and still would harm her not at all. But he shut his teeth, and watched her. Among mountain women the girl was more than pretty; elsewhere only her hair, perhaps, would have caught the casual eye. She wore red homespun and coarse shoes; her hands were brown and hardened. Her arms and shoulders looked muscular, her waist was rather large-being as nature meant it-and her face in repose had a heavy look. But the poise of her head suggested native pride and dignity; her eyes were deep, and full of changing lights; the scarlet dress, loose as it was, showed rich curves in her figure, and her movements had a certain childlike grace. Her brow was low, and her mouth had character; the chin was firm, the upper lip short, and the teeth were even and white.

"I reckon thar's enough to fill the sack, Isom," said the old miller, breaking the strained silence of the group. The girl rose and handed him a few pieces of silver.

I reckon I'd better pay fer it all," she said. I s'pose I won't be over hyeh ag'in."

Old Gabe gave some of the coins back.

"Y'u know whut my price al'ays is," he said.

I'm obleeged," answered the girl, flushing.

"Co'n hev riz on our side. I thought mebbe you charged folks over thar more, anyways."

"I sells fer the same, ef co'n is high ur low," was the answer. "This side or t'other makes no diff'unce to me. I hev frien's on both sides, 'n' I take no part in sech doin's as air a shame to the mountains."

There was a quick light of protest in the girl's dark eyes; but the old miller was honored by both factions, and without a word she turned to the boy, who was tying the sack.

The boat's loose! " he called out, with. the string between his teeth; and she turned again and ran out. Rome stood still.

Kerry the sack out, boy, 'n' holp the gal." Old Gabe's voice was stern, and the young mountaineer doggedly swung the bag to his shoulders. The girl had caught the rope, and drawn the rude dugout along the shore.

"Who axed ye to do that?" she asked, angrily.

Rome dropped the bag into the boat, and merely looked her in the face.

"Look hyeh, Rome Stetson"-the sound of his name from her lips almost startled him-"I'll hev ye understan' that I don't want to be bounden to you, nor none o' yer kin."

Turning, she gave an impatient sweep with her paddle. The prow of the canoe dipped and was motionless. Rome had caught the stern, and the girl wheeled in hot anger. Her impulse to strike may have been for the moment and no longer, or she may have read swiftly no unkindness in the mountaineer's steady look; for the uplifted oar was stayed in the air, as though at least she would hear him.

"I've got nothin' ag'in' you," he said, slowly, Jas Lewallen hev been threatenin' me, 'n' I thought it was him, 'n' I was ready fer him, when you come into the mill. I wouldn't hurt you nur no other woman. Y'u ought to know it, 'n' ye do know it."

The words were masterful, but said in a way that vaguely soothed the girl's pride, and the oar was let slowly into the water.

"I reckon y'u air a friend o' his," he added, still quietly. "I've seed ye goin' up thar, but I've got nothin' ag'in' ye, whoever ye be."

She turned on him a sharp look of suspicion. "I reckon I do be a friend o' hisn," she said, deliberately; and then she saw that he was in earnest. A queer little smile went like a ray of light from her eyes to her lips, and she gave a quick stroke with her paddle. The boat shot into the current, and was carried swiftly toward the Cumberland. The girl stood erect, swaying through light and shadow like a great scarlet flower blowing in the wind; and Rome watched her till she touched the other bank. Swinging the sack out, she stepped lightly after it, and, without looking behind her, disappeared in the bushes.

The boy Isom was riding away when Rome, turned, and old Gabe was watching from the door of the mill.

Who is that gal? " he asked, slowly. It seemed somehow that he had known her a long while ago. A puzzled frown overlay his face, and the old miller laughed.

"You a-axin' who she be, 'n' she a-axin who you be, 'n' both o' ye a-knowin' one 'nother sence ye was knee-high. Why, boy, hit's old Jasper's gal-Marthy!

VI

IN a flash of memory Rome saw the girl as vividly as when he last saw her years ago. They had met at the mill, he with his father, she with hers. There was a quarrel, and the two men were held apart. But the old sore as usual was opened, and a week later Rome's father was killed from the brush. He remembered his mother's rage and grief, her calls for vengeance, the uprising, the fights, plots, and ambushes. He remembered the look the girl had given him that long ago, and her look that day was little changed.

When fighting began, she had been sent for safety to the sister of her dead mother in another county. When peace came, old Jasper married again and the girl refused to come home. Lately the step-mother, too, had passed away, and then she came back to live. All this the old miller told in answer to Rome's questions as the two walked away in the twilight. This was why he had not recognized her, and why her face yet seemed familiar even when he crossed the river that morning.

"Uncle Gabe, how do you reckon the gal knowed who I was?"

"She axed me."

"She axed you! Whar?"

Over thar in the mill." The miller was watching the young mountaineer closely. The manner of the girl was significant when she asked who Rome was, and the miller knew but one reason possible for his foolhardiness that morning.

"Do you mean to say she have been over hyeh afore?"

"Why, yes, come to think about it, three or four times while Isom was sick, and whut she come fer I can't make out. The mill over thar wasn't broke long, 'n' why she didn't go thar or bring more co'n at a time, to save her the trouble o' so many trips, I can't see to save me.

Young Stetson was listening eagerly. Again the miller cast his bait.

Mebbe she's spyin'."

Rome faced him, alert with suspicion; but old Gabe was laughing silently.

"Don't you be a fool, Rome. The gal comes and goes in that boat, 'n' she couldn't see a soul without my knowin' it. She seed ye ridin' by one day, 'n' she looked mighty cur'us when I tole her who ye was."

Old Gabe stopped his teasing, Rome's face was so troubled, and himself grew serious.

"Rome," he said, earnestly, "I wish to the good Lord ye wasn't in sech doin's. Ef that had been young Jas 'stid o' Marthy, I reckon ye would 'a' killed him right thar."

"I wasn't going to let him kill me," was the sullen answer.

The two had stopped at a rickety gate swinging open on the road. The young mountaineer was pushing a stone about with the toe of his boot. He had never before listened to remonstrance with such patience, and old Gabe grew bold.

"You've been drinkin' ag'in, Rome," he said, sharply, " 'n' I know it. Hit's been moonshine that's whooped you Stetsons, not the Lewallens, long as I kin rickollect, 'n' it ull be moonshine ag'in ef ye don't let it alone."

Rome made no denial, no defence. "Uncle Gabe," he said slowly, still busied with the stone, " hev that gal been over hyeh sence y'u tol' her who I was?"

The old man was waiting for the pledge that seemed on his lips, but he did not lose his temper.

Not till to-day," he said, quietly.

Rome turned abruptly, and the two separated with no word of parting. For a moment the miller watched the young fellow striding away under his rifle.

"I have been atter peace a good while," he said to himself, " but I reckon thar's a bigger hand a-workin' now than mine." Then he lifted his voice. "Ef Isom's too sick to come down to the mill to-morrer, I wish you'd come 'n' holp me."

Rome nodded back over his shoulder, and went on, with head bent, along the river road. Passing a clump of pines at the next curve, he pulled a bottle from his pocket.

"Uncle Gabe's about right, I reckon," he said, half aloud; and he raised it above his head to hurl it away, but checked it in mid-air. For a moment he looked at the colorless liquid, then, with quick nervousness, pulled the cork of sassafras leaves, gulped down the pale moonshine, and dashed the bottle against the trunk of a beech. The fiery stuff does its work in a hurry. He was thirsty when he reached the mouth of a brook that tumbled down the mountain along the pathway that would lead him home, and he stooped to drink where the water sparkled in a rift of dim light from overhead. Then he sat upright on a stone, with his wide hat-brim curved in a crescent over his forehead, his hands caught about his knees, and his eyes on the empty air.

He was scarcely over his surprise that the girl was young Lewallen's sister, and the discovery had wrought a curious change. The piquant impulse of rivalry was gone, and something deeper was taking its place. He was confused and a good deal troubled, thinking it all over. He tried to make out what the girl meant by looking at him from the mountain-side, by waving her bonnet at him, and by coming to old Gabe's mill when she could have gone to her own. To be sure, she did not know then who he was, and she had stopped coming when she learned; but why had she crossed again that day? Perhaps she too was bantering him, and he was at once angry and drawn to her; for her mettlesome spirit touched his own love of daring, even when his humiliation was most bitter-when she told him he warred on women; when he held out to her the branch of peace and she swept it aside with a stroke of her oar. But Rome was little conscious of the weight of subtle facts like these. His unseeing eyes went back to her as she combed her hair. He saw the color in her cheeks, the quick light in her eyes, the naked, full throat once more, and the wavering forces of his unsteady brain centred in a stubborn resolution-to see it all again. He would make Isom stay at home, if need be, and he would take the boy's place at the mill. If she came there no more, he would cross the river again. Come peace or war, be she friend or enemy, he would see her. His thirst was fierce again, and, with this half-drunken determination in his heart, he stooped once more to drink from the cheerful little stream. As he rose, a loud curse smote the air. The river, pressed between two projecting cliffs, was narrow at that point, and the oath came across the water. An instant later a man led a lamed horse from behind a bowlder, and stooped to examine its leg. The dusk was thickening, but Rome knew the huge frame and gray beard of old Jasper Lewallen. The blood beat in a sudden tide at his temples, and, half by instinct, he knelt behind a rock, and, thrusting his rifle through a crevice, cocked it softly.

Again the curse of impatience came over the still water, and old Jasper rose and turned toward him. The glistening sight caught in the centre of his beard. That would take him in the throat; it might miss, and he let the sight fall till the bullet would cut the fringe of gray hair into the heart. Old Jasper, so people said, had killed his father in just this way; he had driven his uncle from the mountains; he was trying now to revive the feud. He was the father of young Jasper, who had threatened his life, and the father of the girl whose contempt had cut him to the quick twice that day. Again her taunt leaped through his heated brain, and his boast to the old miller followed it. His finger trembled at the trigger.

"No; by—, no! "he breathed between his teeth; and old Jasper passed on, unharmed.

VII

NEXT day the news of Rufe Stetson's flight went down the river on the wind, and before nightfall the spirit of murder was loosed on both shores of the Cumberland. The more cautious warned old Jasper. The Stetsons were gaining strength again, they said; so were their feudsmen, the Marcums, enemies of the Braytons, old Jasper's kinspeople. Keeping store, Rufe had made money in the West, and money and friends right and left through the mountains. With all his good-nature, he was a persistent hater, and he was shrewd. He had waited the chance to put himself on the side of the law, and now the law was with him. But old Jasper laughed contemptuously. Rufe Stetson was gone again, he said, as he had gone before, and this time for good. Rufe had tried to do what nobody had done, or could do, while he was alive. Anyway, he was reckless, and he cared little if war did come again. Still, the old man prepared for a fight, and Steve Marcum on the other shore made ready for Rufe's return.

It was like the breaking of peace in feudal days. The close kin of each leader were already about him, and now the close friends of each took sides. Each leader trading in Hazlan had debtors scattered through the mountains, and these rallied to aid the man who had befriended them. There was no grudge but served a pretext for partisanship in the coming war. Political rivalry had wedged apart two strong families, the Marcums and Braytons; a boundary line in dispute was a chain of bitterness; a suit in a country court had sown seeds of hatred. Sometimes it was a horse-trade, a fence left down, or a gate left open, and the trespassing of cattle; in one instance, through spite, a neighbor had docked the tail of a neighbor's horse-had " muled his critter," as the owner phrased the outrage. There was no old sore that was not opened by the crafty leaders, no slumbering bitterness that they did not wake to life. " Help us to revenge, and we will he!p you," was the whispered promise. So, had one man a grudge against another, he could set his foot on one or the other shore, sure that his enemy would be fighting for the other.

Others there were, friends of neither leader, who, under stress of poverty or hatred of work, would fight with either for food and clothes; and others still, the ne'er-do-wells and outlaws, who fought by the day or month for hire. Even these were secured by one or the other faction, for Steve and old Jasper left no resource untried, knowing well that the fight, if there was one, would be fought to a quick and decisive end. The day for the leisurely feud, for patient planning, and the slow picking off of men from one side or the other, was gone. The people in the Blue Grass, who had no feuds in their own country, were trying to stop them in the mountain. Over in Breathitt, as everybody knew, soldiers had come from the " settlemints," had arrested the leaders, and had taken them to the Blue Grass for the feared and hated ordeal of trial by a jury of "bigoted furriners." On the heels of the soldiers came a young preacher up from the Jellico hills, half " citizen," half furriner," with long black hair and a scar across his forehead, who was stirring up the people, it was said, " as though Satan was atter them." Over there the spirit of the feud was broken, and a good effect was already perceptible around Hazlan. In past days every pair of lips was sealed with fear, and the non-combatants left crops and homes, and moved down the river, when trouble began. Now only the timid considered this way of escape. Steve and old Jasper found a few men who refused to enter the fight. Several, indeed, talked openly against the renewal of the feud, and somebody, it was said, had dared to hint that he would send to the Governor for aid if it should break out again. But these were rumors touching few people.

For once again, as time and time again before, one bank of the Cumberland was arrayed with mortal enmity against the other, and old Gabe sat, with shaken faith, in the door of his mill. For years he had worked and prayed for peace, and for a little while the Almighty seemed lending aid. Now the friendly grasp was loosening, and yet the miller did all he could. He begged Steve Marcum to urge Rufe to seek aid from the law when the latter came back; and Steve laughed, and asked what justice was possible for a Stetson, with a Lewallen for a judge and Braytons for a jury. The miller pleaded with old Jasper, and old Jasper pointed to the successes of his own life.

"I hev triumphed ag'in' my enemies time 'n' ag'in," he said. "The Lord air on my side, 'n' I gits a better Christian ever' year." The old man spoke with the sincerity of a barbarism that has survived the dark ages, and, holding the same faith, the miller had no answer. It was old Gabe indeed who had threatened to send to the Governor for soldiers, and this he would have done, perhaps, had there not been one hope left, and only one. A week had gone, and there was no word from Rufe Stetson. Up on Thunderstruck Knob the old Stetson mother was growing pitiably eager and restless. Every day she slipped like a ghost through the leafless woods and in and out the cabin, kindling hatred. At every dawn or dusk she was on her porch peering through the dim light for Rufe Stetson. Steve Marcum was ill at ease. Rome Stetson alone seemed unconcerned, and his name was on every gossiping tongue.

He took little interest and no hand in getting ready for the war. He forbade the firing of a gun till Rufe came back, else Steve should fight his fight alone. He grew sullen and morose. His old mother's look was a thorn in his soul, and he stayed little at home. He hung about the mill, and when Isom became bedfast, the big mountaineer, who had never handled anything but a horse, a plough, or a rifle, settled him-self, to the bewilderment of the Stetsons, into the boy's duties, and nobody dared question him. Even old Gabe jested no longer. The matter was too serious.

Meanwhile the winter threw off the last slumbrous mood of autumn, as a sleeper starts from a dream. A fortnight was gone, and still no message came from the absent leader. One shore was restive, uneasy; the other confident, mocking. Between the two, Rome Stetson waited his chance at the mill.

VIII

DAY was whitening on the Stetson shore. Across the river the air was still sharp with the chill of dawn, and the mists lay like flocks of sheep under shelter of rock and crag. A peculiar cry radiated from the Lewallen cabin with singular resonance on the crisp air-the mountain cry for straying cattle. A soft low came from a distant patch of laurel, and old Jasper's girl, Martha, folded. her hands like a conch at her mouth, and the shrill cry again startled the air.

Ye better come, ye pieded cow-brute." Picking up a cedar piggin, she stepped from the porch toward the meek voice that had answered her. Temper and exertion had brought the quick blood to her face. Her head was bare, her thick hair was loosely coiled, and her brown arms were naked almost to the shoulder. At the stable a young mountaineer was overhauling his riding-gear.

Air you goin' to ride the hoss to-day, Jas?" she asked, querulously.

"That's jes whut I was aimin' to do. I'm a-goin' to town."

Well, I 'lowed I was goin' to mill to-day. The co'n is 'mos' gone."

"Well, y'u 'lowed wrong," he answered, imperturbably.

Y'u're mean, Jas Lewallen," she cried, hotly; " that's whut ye air, mean-dog-mean!

The young mountaineer looked up, whistled softly, and laughed. But when he brought his horse to the door an hour later there was a bag of corn across the saddle.

"As ye air so powerful sot on goin' to mill, whether or no, I'll leave this hyeh sack at the bend O' the road, 'n' ye kin git it thar. I'll bring the meal back ef ye puts it in the same place. I hates to see women-folks a-ridin' this horse. Hit spiles him."

The horse was a dapple-gray of unusual beauty, and as the girl reached out her hand to stroke his throat, he turned to nibble at her arm.

"I reckon he'd jes as lieve have me ride him as you, Jas," she said. " Me 'n' him have got to be great friends. Ye orter n't to be so stingy."

Well, he ain't no hoss to be left out'n the bresh now, 'n' I hain't goin' to 'low it."

Old Jasper had lounged out of the kitchen door, and stood with his huge bulk against a shrinking pillar of the porch. The two men were much alike. Both had the same black, threatening brows meeting over the bridge of the nose. A kind of grim humor lurked about the old man's mouth, which time might trace about young Jasper's. The girl's face had no humor; the same square brows, apart and clearly marked, gave it a strong, serious cast, and while she had the Lewallen fire, she favored her mother enough, so the neighbors said, "to have a mighty mild, takin' way about her ef she wanted."

You're right, Jas," the old mountaineer said; "the hoss air a sin 'n' temptation. Hit do me good ever' time I look at him. Thar air no sech hoss, I tell ye, this side o' the settlements."

The boy started away, and the old man followed, and halted him out of the girl's hearing.

"Tell Eli Crump 'n' Jim Stover to watch the Breathitt road close now," he said, in a low voice. " See all them citizens I tol' ye, 'n' tell 'em to be ready when I says the word. Thar's no tellin' whut's goin' to happen."

Young Jasper nodded his head, and struck his horse into a gallop. The old man lighted his pipe, and turned back to the house. The girl, bonnet in hand, was starting for the valley.

"Thar ain't no use goin' to Gabe Bunch's fer yer grist," he said. " The mill on Dead Crick's a-runnin' ag'in, 'n' I don't want ye over thar axin favors, specially jes now."

"I lef' somethin' fer ye to eat, dad," she replied, " ef ye gits hungry before I git back."

You heerd me? " he called after her, knitting his brows.

Yes, dad; I heerd ye," she answered, adding to herself, " But I don't heed ye." In truth, the girl heeded nobody. It was not her way to ask consent, even her own, nor to follow advice. At the bend of the road she found the bag, and for an instant she stood wavering. An impulse turned her to the river, and she loosed the boat, and headed it across the swift, shallow water from the ford and straight toward the mill. At every stroke of her paddle the water rose above the prow of the boat, and, blown into spray, flew back and drenched her; the wind loosed her hair, and, tugging at her skirts, draped her like a statue; and she fought them, wind and water, with mouth set and a smile in her eyes. One sharp struggle still, where the creek leaped into freedom; the mouth grew a little firmer, the eyes laughed more, the keel grated on pebbles, and the boat ran its nose into the withered sedge on the Stetson shore.

A tall gray figure was pouring grain into the hopper when she reached the door of the mill. She stopped abruptly, Rome Stetson turned, and again the two were face to face. No greeting passed. The girl lifted her head with a little toss that deepened the set look about the mountaineer's mouth; her lax figure grew tense as though strung suddenly against some coming harm, and her eyes searched the shadows without once resting on him.

Whar's Uncle Gabe? " She spoke shortly, and as to a stranger.

Gone to town," said Rome, composedly. He had schooled himself for this meeting.

When's he comm' back?

Not 'fore night, I reckon."

Whar's Isom?

Isom's sick."

Well, who's tendin' this mill?

For answer he tossed the empty bag into the corner and, without looking at her, picked up another bag.

"I reckon ye see me, don't ye? " he asked, coolly. " Hev a cheer, and rest a spell. Hit's a purty long climb whar you come from."

The girl was confused. She stayed in the doorway, a little helpless and suspicious. What was Rome Stetson doing here? His mastery of the situation, his easy confidence, puzzled and irritated her. Should she leave? The mountaineer was a Stetson, a worm to tread on if it crawled across the path. It would be like backing down before an enemy. He might laugh at her after she was gone, and, at that thought, she sat down in the chair with composed face, looking through the door at the tumbling water, which broke with a thousand tints under the sun, but able still to see Rome, sidewise, as he moved about the hopper, whistling softly.

Once she looked around, fancying she saw a smile on his sober face. Their eyes came near meeting, and she turned quite away.

Ever seed a body out'n his head?

The girl's eyes rounded with a start of surprise.

Well, it's plumb cur'us. Isom's been that way lately. Isom's sick, ye know. Uncle Gabe's got the rheumatiz, 'n' Isom's mighty fond o' Uncle Gabe, 'n' the boy pestered me till I come down to he'p him. Hit p'int'ly air strange to hear him talkin'. He's jes a-ravin' 'bout hell 'n' heaven, 'n' the sin o' killin' folks. You'd ha' thought he hed been convicted, though none o' our fambly hev been much atter religion. He says as how the wrath uv a livin' God is a-goin' to sweep these mount ins, ef some mighty tall repentin' hain't done. Of co'se he got all them notions from Gabe. But Isom al'ays was quar, 'n' seed things hisself. He ain't no fool!"

The girl was listening. Morbidly sensitive to the supernatural, she had turned toward him, and her face was relaxed with fear and awe.

"He's havin' dreams 'n' sech-like now, 'n' I reckon thar's nothing he's seed or heerd that he don' talk about. He's been a-goin' on about you," he added, abruptly. The girl's hands gave a nervous twitch. "Oh, he don't say nothin' ag'in' ye. I reckon he tuk a fancy to ye. Mam was plumb distracted, not knowin' whar he had seed ye. She thought it was like his other talk, 'n' I never let on-a-knowin' how mam was." A flush rose like a flame from the girl's throat to her hair. " But hit's this," Rome went on in an unsteady tone, "that he talks most about, 'n' I'm sorry myself that trouble's a-comm'." He dropped all pretence now. "I've been a-watchin' fer ye over thar on t' other shore a good deal lately. I didn't know ye at fust, Marthy "-he spoke her name for the first time-' 'n' Gabe says y'u didn't know me. I remembered ye, though, 'n' I want to tell ye now what I tol' ye then: I've got nothin' ag'in you. I was hopin' ye mought come over ag'in-hit was sorter cur'us that y'u was the same gal-the same gal-"

His self-control left him; he was halting in speech, and blundering he did not know where. Fumbling an empty bag at the hopper, he had not dared to look at the girl till he heard her move. She had risen, and was picking up her bag. The hard antagonism of her face calmed him instantly.

Hain't ye goin' to have yer grist ground?

Not hyeh," she answered, quickly.

"Why, gal	" He got no further. Martha was gone, and he followed her to the bank, bewildered.

The girl's suspicion, lulled by his plausible explanation, had grown sharp again. The mountaineer knew that she had been coming there. He was at the mill for another reason than to take the boy's place; and with swift in-tuition she saw the truth.

He got angry as she rode away-angry with himself that he had let her go; and the same half-tender, half-brutal impulse seized him as when he saw her first. This time he yielded. His horse was at hand, and the river not far below was narrow. The bridle-path that led to the Lewallen cabin swerved at one place to a cliff over-looking the river, and by hard riding and a climb of a few hundred feet on foot he could overtake her half-way up the mountain steep.

The plan was no more than shaped before he was in the saddle and galloping down the river. The set of his face changed hardly a line while he swam the stream, and, drenched to the waist, scaled the cliff. When he reached the spot, he found the prints of a woman's shoe in the dust of the path, going down. There were none returning, and he had not long to wait. A scarlet bit of color soon flashed through the gray bushes below him. The girl was without her bag of corn. She was climbing slowly, and was looking at the ground as though in deep thought. Reckless as she was, she had come to realize at last just what she had done. She had been pleased at first, as would have been any woman, when she saw the big mountaineer watching her, for her life was lonely. She had waved her bonnet at him from mere mischief. She hardly knew it herself, but she had gone across the river to find out who he was. She had shrunk from him as from a snake thereafter, and had gone no more until old Jasper had sent her because the Lewallen mill was broken, and because she was a woman, and would be safe from harm. She had met him then when she could not help herself. But now she had gone of her own accord. She had given this Stetson, a bitter enemy, a chance to see her, to talk with her. She had listened to him; she had been on the point of letting him grind her corn. And he knew how often she had gone to the mill, and he could not know that she had ever been sent. Perhaps he thought that she had come to make overtures of peace, friendship, even more. The suspicion reddened her face with shame, and her anger at him was turned upon herself. Why she had gone again that day she hardly knew. But if there was another reason than simple perversity, it was the memory of Rome Stetson's face when he caught her boat and spoke to her in a way she could not answer. The anger of the moment came with every thought of the incident afterward, and with it came too this memory of his look, which made her at once defiant and uneasy. She saw him now only when she was quite close, and, startled, she stood still; his stern look brought her the same disquiet, but she gave no sign of fear.

Whut's the matter with ye?

The question was too abrupt, too savage, and the girl looked straight at him, and her lips tightened with a resolution not to speak. The movement put him beyond control.

"Y'u puts hell into me, Marthy Lewallen; y'u puts downright hell into me." The words came between gritted teeth. "I want to take ye up 'n' throw ye off this cliff clean into the river, 'n' I reckon the next minute I'd jump off atter ye. Y'u've 'witched me, gal! I forgits who ye air 'n' who I be, 'n' sometimes I want to come over hyeh 'n' kerry ye out'n these mount ins, n' nuver come back. You know whut I've been watchin' the river fer sence the fust time I seed ye. You know whut I've been a-stayin' at the mill fer, 'n' Steve mad 'n' mam a-jowerin'-'n' a-lookin' over hyeh fer ye night 'n' day! Y'u know whut I've jes swum over hyeh fer! Whut's the matter with ye?"

Martha was not looking for a confession like this. It took away her shame at once, and the passion of it thrilled her, and left her trembling. While he spoke her lashes drooped quickly, her face softened, and the color came back to it. She began intertwining her fingers, and would not look up at him.

Ef y'u hates me like the rest uv ye, why don't ye say it right out? 'N' ef ye do hate me, whut hev you been lookin' 'cross the river fer, 'n' a-shakin' yer bonnet at me, 'n' paddlin' to Gabe's fer yer grist, when the mill on Dead Crick's been a-runnin', 'n' I know it? You've been banterin' me, hev ye? "-the blood rose to his eyes again. " Ye mustn't fool with me, gal, by , ye mustn't. Whut hev you been goin' over thar fer? " He even took a threatening step toward her, and, with a helpless gesture, stopped. The girl was a little frightened. Indeed, she smiled, seeing her power over him; she seemed even about to laugh outright; but the smile turned to a quick look of alarm, and she bent her head suddenly to listen to something below. At last she did speak. "Somebody's comm'! " she said. " You'd better git out O' the way," she went on, hurriedly. "Somebody's comm', I tell ye! Don't ye hear?

It was no ruse to get rid of him. The girl's eyes were dilating. Something was coming far below. Rome could catch the faint beats of a horse's hoofs. He was un-armed, and he knew it was death for him to be seen on that forbidden mountain; but he was beyond caution, and ready to welcome any vent to his passion, and he merely shook his head.

Ef it's Satan hisself, I hain't goin' to run." The hoof-beats came nearer. The rider must soon see them from the coil below.

Rome, hit's Jas! He's got his rifle, and he'll kill ye, 'n' me too! " The girl was white with distress. She had called him by his name, and the tone was of appeal, not anger. The black look passed from his face, and he caught her by the shoulders with rough tenderness; but she pushed him away, and without a word he sprang from the road and let himself noiselessly down the cliff. The hoof-beats thundered above his head, and Young Jasper's voice hailed Martha.

This hyeh's the bigges' meal I ever straddled. Why d'n't ye git the grist ground?"

For a moment the girl did not answer, and Rome waited, breathless. " Wasn't the mill runnin'? Whyn't ye go on 'cross the river?

That's whut I did," said the girl, quietly. Uncle Gabe wasn't thar, 'n' Rome Stetson was. I wouldn't 'low him to grin' the co 'n, 'n' so I toted hit back."

Rome Stetson! " The voice was lost in a volley of oaths.

The two passed out of hearing, and Rome went plunging down the mountain, swinging recklessly from one little tree to another, and wrenching limbs from their sockets out of pure physical ecstasy. When he reached his horse he sat down, breathing heavily, on a bed of moss, with a strange new yearning in his heart. If peace should come! Why not peace, if Rufe should not come back? He would be the leader then, and without him there could be no war. Old Jasper had killed his father. He was too young at the time to feel poignant sorrow now, and somehow he could look even at that death in a fairer way. His father had killed old Jasper's brother. So it went back: a Lewallen killed a Stetson; that Stetson had killed a

Lewallen, until one end of the chain of deaths was lost, and the first fault could not be placed, though each clan put it on the other. In every generation there had been compromises- periods of peace; why not now? Old Gabe would gladly help him. He might make friends with young Jasper; he might even end the feud. And then-he and Martha-why not? He closed his eyes, and for one radiant moment t all seemed possible. And then a gaunt image rose in the dream, and only the image was left. It was the figure of his mother, stern and silent through the years, opening her grim lips rarely without some curse against the Lewallen race. He remembered she had smiled for the first time when she heard of the new trouble-the flight of his uncle and the hope of conflict. She had turned to him with her eyes on fire and her old hands clinched. She had said nothing, but he understood her look. And now- Good God! what would she think and say if she could know what he had done? His whole frame twitched at the thought, and, with a nervous spring to escape it, he was on his feet, and starting down the mountain.

Close to the river he heard voices below him, and he turned his horse quickly aside into the bushes. Two women who had been washing clothes passed, carrying white bundles home. They were talking of the coming feud.

"That ar young Stetson ain't much like his dad," said one. "Young Jas has been a-darin' 'n' a-banterin' him, 'n' he won't take it up. They say he air turnin' out a plumb coward."

When he reached the Stetson cabin three horses with drooping heads were hitched to the fence. All had travelled a long way. One wore a man's saddle; on the others were thick blankets tied together with leathern thongs.

In the dark porch sat several men. Through the kitchen door he could see his mother getting supper. Inside a dozen rifles leaned against the wall in the fire-light, and about their butts was a pile of ammunition. In the doorway stood Rufe Stetson.

IX

ALL were smoking and silent. Several spoke from the shadows as Rome stepped on the porch, and Rufe Stetson faced him a moment in the door-way, and laughed.

Seem kinder s'prised? " he said, with a searching look. " Wasn't lookin' for me? I reckon I'll s'prise sev'ral ef I hev good-luck."

The subtlety of this sent a chuckle of appreciation through the porch, but Rome passed in without answer.

Isom lay on his bed within the circle of light, and his face in the brilliant glow was white, and his eyes shone feverishly. " Rome," he said, excitedly, " Uncle Rufe's hyeh, 'n' they laywayed him, 'n'____" He paused abruptly. His mother came in, and at her call the mountaineers trooped through the covered porch, and sat down to supper in the kitchen. They ate hastily and in silence, the mother attending their wants, and Rome helping her. The meal finished, they drew their chairs about the fire. Pipes were lighted, and Rufe Stetson rose and closed the door.

Thar's no use harryin' the boy," he said; "I reckon he'll be too puny to take a hand."

The mother stopped clearing the table, and sat on the rock hearth close to the fire, her withered lips shut tight about a lighted pipe, and her sunken eyes glowing like the coal of fire in its black bowl. Now and then she would stretch her knotted hands nervously into the flames, or knit them about her knees, looking closely at the heavy faces about her, which had lightened a little with expectancy. Rufe Stetson stood before the blaze, his hands clasped behind him, and his huge figure bent in reflection. At intervals he would look with half-shut eyes at Rome, who Sat with troubled face outside the firelight. Across the knees of Steve Marcum, the best marksman in the mountains, lay the barrel of a new Winchester. Old Sam

Day, Rufe's father-in-law and counsellor to the Stetsons for a score of years, sat as if asleep on the opposite side of the fireplace from the old mother, with his big square head pressed down between his misshapen shoulders.

"The time hev come, Rome." Rufe spoke between the puffs of his pipe, and Rome's heart quickened, for every eye was upon him. Thar's goin' to be trouble now. I hear as how young Jasper hev been talkin' purty tall about ye-'lowin' as how ye air afeard O' him."

Rome felt his mother's burning look. He did not turn toward her nor Rufe, but his face grew sullen, and his voice was low and harsh. "I reckon he'll find out about that when the time comes," he said, quietly-too quietly, for the old mother stirred uneasily, and significant glances went from eye to eye. Rufe did not look up from the floor. He had been told about Rome's peculiar conduct, and, while the reason for it was beyond guessing, he knew the temper of the boy and how to kindle it. He had thrust a thorn in a tender spot, and he let it rankle. How sorely it did rankle he little knew. The voice of the woman across the river was still in Rome 5 ears. Nothing cuts the mountaineer to the quick like the name of coward. It stung him like the lash of an ox-whip then; it smarted all the way across the river and up the mountain. Young Jasper had been charging him broadcast with cowardice, and Jasper's people no doubt believed it. Perhaps his own did -his uncle, his mother. The bare chance of such a humiliation set up an inward rage. He wondered how he could ever have been such a fool as to think of peace. The woman's gossip had swept kindly impulses from his heart with a fresh tide of bitterness, and, helpless now against its current, he sullenly gave way, and let his passions loose to drift with it.

"Whar d' ye git the guns, Rufe? " Steve was testing the action of the Winchester with a kindling look, as the click of the locks struck softly through the silence.

"Jackson; 'way up in Breathitt, at the eend of the new road."

"No wonder y'u've been gone so long."

"I had to wait thar fer the guns, 'n' I had to travel atter dark comm' back, 'n' lay out'n the bresh by day. Hit's full eighty mile up thar."

"Air ye shore nobody seed ye?"

The question was from a Marcum, who had come in late, and several laughed. Rufe threw back his dusty coat, which was ripped through the lapel by a bullet.

They seed me well 'nough fer that," he said, grimly, and then he looked toward

Rome, who thought of old Jasper, and gave back a gleam of fierce sympathy. There were several nods of approval along with the laugh that followed. It was a surprise- so little consideration of an escape so narrow-from Rufe; for, as old Gabe said, Rufe was big and good-natured, and was not thought fit for leadership. But there was a change in him when he came back from the West. He was quieter; he laughed less No one spoke of the difference; it was too vague; but every one felt it, and it had an effect. His flight had made many uneasy, but his return, for that reason, brought a stancher fealty from these; and this was evident now. All eyes were upon him, and all tongues, even old Sam's, waited now for his to speak.

"Whut we've got to do, we've got to do mighty quick," he began, at last. " Things air changin'. I seed it over thar in Breathitt. The soldiers 'n' that scar- faced Jellico preacher hev broke up the fightin' over thar, 'n' ef we don't watch out, they'll be a-doin' it hyeh, when we start our leetle frolic. We hain't got no time to fool. Old Jas knows this as well as me, 'n' thar's goin' to be mighty leetle chance fer 'em to layway 'n' pick us off from the bresh. Thar's goin' to be fa'r fightin' fer once, thank the Lord. They bushwhacked us dunn' the war, 'n' they've laywayed us 'n' shot us to pieces ever sence; but now, ef God A'mighty's willin', the thing's a-goin' to be settled one way or t'other at last, I reckon."

He stopped a moment to think. The men's breathing could be heard, so quiet was the room, and Rufe went on telling in detail, slowly, as if to himself, the wrongs the Lewallens had done his people. When he came to old Jasper his voice was low, and his manner was quieter than ever.

"Now old Jas have got to the p'int whar he says as how nobody in this county kin undersell him 'n' stay hyeh. Old Jas druv Bond Vickers out'n the mount 'ins fer tryin' hit. He druv Jess Hale away; 'n' them two air our kin."

The big mountaineer turned then, and knocked the ashes from his pipe. His eyes grew a little brighter, and his nostrils spread, but with a sweep of his arm he added, still quietly:

"Y' all know whut he's done."

The gesture lighted memories of personal wrongs in every breast; he had tossed a fire-brand among fagots, and an angry light began to burn from the eyes that watched him.

"Ye know, too, that he thinks he has played the same game with me; but ye don't know, I reckon, that he had ole Jim Stover 'n' that mis'-able Eli Crump a-hidin' in the bushes to shoot me "-again he grasped the torn lapel; "that a body warned me to git away from Hazlan; n' the night I left home they come thar to kill me, 'n' s'arched the house, 'n' skeered Mollie n' the leetle gal 'most to death."

The mountaineer's self-control was lost suddenly in a furious oath. The men did know, but in fresh anger they leaned forward in their chairs, and twisted about with smothered curses. The old woman had stopped smoking, and was rocking her body to and fro. Her lips were drawn in upon her toothless gums, and her pipe was clinched against her sunken breast. The head of the old mountaineer was lifted, and his eyes were open and shining fiercely.

"I hear as how he says I'm gone fer good. Well, I have been kinder easy-goin', hatin' to fight, but sence the day I seed Rome's dad thar dead in his blood, I hev had jes one thing I wanted to do. Thar wasn't no use stayin' hyeh; I seed that. Rome thar was too leetle, and they was too many fer me. I knowed it was easier to git a new start out West, 'n' when I come back to the mount'in, hit was to do jes-whut I'm - going - to - do - now." He wheeled suddenly upon Rome, with one huge hand lifted. Under it the old woman's voice rose in a sudden wail:

Yes; 'n' I want to see it done befoh I die. I hain't hyeh fer long, but I hain't goin' to leave as long as ole Jas is hyeh, 'n' I want ye all to know it. Ole Jas hev got to go fust. You hear me, Rome? I'm a-talkin' to you; I'm a-talkin' to you. Hit's yo' time now!

The frenzied chant raised Rome from his chair. Rufe himself took up the spirit of it, and his voice was above all caution.

"Yes, Rome! They killed him, boy. They sneaked on him, 'n' shot him to pieces from the bushes. Yes; hit's yo' time now! Look hyeh, boys! " He reached above the fireplace and took down an old rifle-his brother's-which the old mother had suffered no one to touch. He held it before the fire, pointing to two crosses made near the flash-pan. " Thar's one fer ole Jim Lewallen! Thar's one fer ole Jas! He got Jim, but ole Jas has got him, 'n' thar's his cross thar yit! Whar's yo' gun, Rome? Shame on ye, boy!"

The wild-eyed old woman was before him. She had divined Rufe's purpose, and was already at his side, with Rome's Winchester in one hand and a clasp-knife in the other. Every man was on his feet; the door was open, and the boy Isom was at the threshold, his eyes blazing from his whitc face. Rome had strode forward.

Yes, boy; now's the time, right hyeh before us all!

The mother had the knife outstretched. Rome took it, and the scratch of the point on the hard steel went twice through the stillness-one more fer the young un"; the voice was the old mother's-then twice again.

The moon was sinking when Rome stood in the door alone. The tramp of horses was growing fainter down the mountain. The trees were swaying in the wind below him, and he could just see the gray cliffs on the other shore. The morning seemed far away; it made him dizzy looking back to it through the tumult of the day. Somewhere in the haze was the vision of a girl's white face-white with distress for him. Her father and her brother he had sworn to kill. He had made a cross for each, and each cross was an oath. He closed the door; and then he gave way, and sat down with his head in both hands. The noises in the kitchen ceased. The fire died away, and the chill air gathered about him. When he rose, the restless eyes of the boy were upon him from the shadows.

X

IT was court-day in Hazlan, but so early in the morning nothing was astir in the town that hinted of its life on such a day. But for the ring of a blacksmith's anvil on the quiet air, and the fact that nowhere was a church-spire visible, a stranger would have thought that the peace of Sabbath overlay a village of God-fearing people. A burly figure lounged in the porch of a rickety house, and yawned under a swinging sign, the rude letters of which promised" private entertainment " for the traveller unlucky enough to pass that way. In the one long, narrow main street, closely flanked by log and framed houses, nothing else human was in sight. Out from this street, and in an empty square, stood the one brick building in the place, the court-house, brick without, brick within; unfinished, unpencilled, unpainted; panes out of the windows, a shutter off here and there, or swinging drunkenly on one hinge; the door wide op en, as though there was no privacy within-a poor structure, with the look of a good man gone shiftless and fast going wrong.

Soon two or three lank brown figures appeared from each direction on foot; then a horseman or two, and by and by mountaineers came in groups, on horse and on foot. In time the side alleys and the court-house square were filled with horses and mules, and even steers. The mountaineers crowded the narrow street: idling from side to side; squatting for a bargain on the wooden sidewalks; grouping on the porch of the rickety hotel, and on the court-house steps loitering in and out of the one store in sight. Out in the street several stood about a horse, looking at his teeth, holding his eyes to the sun, punching his ribs, twisting his tail; while the phlegmatic owner sat astride the submissive beast, and spoke short answers to rare questions. Everybody talked politics, the crop failure, or the last fight at the seat of some private war; but nobody spoke of a Lewallen or a Stetson unless he knew his listener's heart, and said it in a whisper. For nobody knew when the powder would flash, or who had taken sides, or that a careless word might not array him with one or the other faction.

A motley throng it was-in brown or gray homespun, with trousers in cowhide boots, and slouched hats with brims curved according to temperament, but with striking figures in it; the patriarch with long, white hair, shorn even with the base of the neck, and bearded only at the throat-a justice of the peace, and the sage of his district; a little mountaineer with curling black hair and beard, and dark, fine features; a grizzled giant with a head rugged enough to have been carelessly chipped from stone; a bragging candidate claiming everybody's notice; a square-shouldered fellow surging through the crowd like a stranger; an open-faced, devil-may- care young gallant on fire with moonshine; a skulking figure with brutish mouth and shifting eyes. Indeed, every figure seemed distinct; for, living apart from his neighbor, and troubling the law but little in small matters of dispute, the mountaineer preserves independence, and keeps the edges of his individuality un-worn. Apparently there was not a woman in town. Those that lived there kept housed, and the fact was significant. Still, it was close to noon, and yet not a Stetson or a Lewallen had been seen. The stores of Rufe and old Jasper were at the extremi-ties of the town, and the crowd did not move those ways. It waited in the centre, and whetted impatience by sly trips in twos and three to stables or side alleys for "mountain dew." Now and then the sheriff, a little man with a mighty voice, would appear on the courthouse steps, and summon a witness to court, where a frightened judge gave instructions to a frightened jury. But few went, unless called; for the interest was outside; every man in the streets knew that a storm was nigh, and was waiting to see it burst.

Noon passed. A hoarse bell and a whining hound had announced dinner in the hotel. The guests were coming again into the streets. Eyes were brighter, faces a little more flushed, and the "moonshine" was passed more openly. Both ways the crowd watched closely. The quiet at each end of the street was ominous, and the delay could last but little longer. The lookers-on themselves were getting quarrel-some. The vent must come soon, or among them there would be trouble.

Thar comes Jas Lewallen! " At last. A dozen voices spoke at once. A horseman had appeared far down the street from the Lewallen end. The clouds broke from about the sun, and a dozen men knew the horse that bore him; for the gray was prancing the street sidewise, and throwing the sunlight from his flanks. Nobody followed, and the crowd was puzzled. Young Jasper carried a Winchester across his saddle-bow, and, swaying with the action of his horse, came on.

"What air he about?"

"He's a plumb idgit."

He mus' be crazy."

He's drunk!

The wonder ceased. Young Jasper was reeling. Two or three Stetsons slipped from the crowd, and there was a galloping of hoofs the other way. Another horseman appeared from the Lewallen end, riding hastily. The new-comer's errand was to call Jasper back. But the young dare-devil was close to the crowd, and was swinging a bottle over his head.

Come back hyeh, Jas! Come hyeh!" The new-comer was shouting afar off while he galloped. Horses were being untethered from the side alleys. Several more Lewallen riders came in sight. They could see the gray shining in the sunlight amid the crowd, and the man sent after him halted at a safe distance, gesticulating; and they, too, spurred forward.

Hello, boys! " young Jasper was calling out, as he swayed from side to side, the people everywhere giving him way.

"Fun to-day, by- ! fun to-day! Who'll hev a drink? Hyeh's hell to the Stetsons, whar some of 'em '11 be afore night!

With a swagger he lifted the bottle to his lips, and, stopping short, let it fall untouched to the ground. He had straightened in his saddle, and was looking up the street. With a deep curse he threw the Winchester to his shoulder, fired, and before his yell had died on his lips horse and rider were away like a shaft of light. The crowd melted like magic from the street. The Stetsons, chiefly on foot, did not return the fire, but halted up the street, as if parleying. Young Jasper joined his party, and they, too, stood still a moment, puzzled by the irresolution of the other side.

"Watch out! they're gittin' round ye! Run for the court-house, ye fools !-ye, run! " The voice came in a loud yell from somewhere down the street, and its warning was just in time.

A wreath of smoke came about a corner of the house far down the street, and young Jasper yelled, and dashed up a side alley with his followers. A moment later judge, jury, witnesses, and sheriff were flying down the court-house steps at the point of Lewallen guns; the Lewallen horses, led by the gray, were snorting through the streets; their riders, barricaded in the forsaken court-house, were puffing a stream of fire and smoke from every window of court-room below and jury-room above.

The streets were a bedlam. The Stetsons were yelling with triumph. The Lewallens were divided, and Rufe placed three Stetsons with Winchesters on each side of the courthouse, and kept them firing. Rome, pale and stern, hid his force between the square and the Lewallen store. He was none too quick. The rest were coming on, led by old Jasper. It was reckless, riding that way right into death; but the old man believed young Jasper's life at stake, and the men behind asked no questions when old Jasper led them. The horses' hoofs beat the dirt street like the crescendo of thunder. The fierce old man's hat was gone, and his mane-like hair was shaking in the wind. Louder-and still the Stetsons were quiet-quiet too long. The wily old man saw the trap, and, with a yell, whirled the column up an alley, each man flattening over his saddle. From every window, from behind every corner and tree, smoke belched from the mouth of a Winchester. Two horses went down; one screamed; the other struggled to his feet, and limped away with an empty saddle. One pf the fallen men sprang into safety behind a house, and one lay still, with his arms stretched out and his face in the dust.

From behind barn, house, and fence the Lewallens gave back a scattering fire; but the Stetsons crept closer, and were plainly in greater numbers. Old Jasper was being surrounded, and he mounted again, and all, followed by a chorus of bullets and triumphant yells, fled for a wooded slope in the rear of the court-house. A dozen Lewallens were prisoners, and must give up or starve. There was savage joy in the Stetson crowd, and many-footed rumor went all ways that night.

Despite sickness and Rome's strict order, Isom had ridden down to the mill. Standing in the doorway, he and old Gabe saw up the river, where the water broke into foam over the ford, a riderless gray horse plunging across. Later it neighed at a gate under Wolf's Head, and Martha Lewallen ran out to meet it. Across under Thunderstruck Knob that night the old Stetson mother listened to Isom's story of the fight with ghastly joy in her death-marked face.

XI

ALL night the court-house was guarded and on guard. At one corner of the square Rufe Stetson, with a few men, sat on watch in old Sam Day's cabin-the fortress of the town, built for such a purpose, and used for it many times before. The prisoners, too, were alert, and no Stetson ventured into the open square, for the moon was high; an exposure anywhere was noted instantly by the whistle of a rifle-ball, and the mountaineer takes few risks except under stress of drink or passion. Rome Stetson had placed pickets about the town wherever surprise was possible. All night he patrolled the streets to keep his men in such readiness as he could for the attack that the Lewallens would surely make to rescue their living friends and to avenge the dead ones.

But the triumph was too great and unexpected. Two Braytons were dead; several more were prisoners with young Jasper in the courthouse; and drinking began.

As the night deepened without attack the Stetsons drank more, and grew reckless. A dance was started. Music and "moonshine" were given to every man who bore a Winchester. The night was broken with drunken yells, the random discharge of fire-arms, and the mono-tone of heavy feet. The two leaders were helpless, and the inaction of the Lewallens puzzled them. Chafed with anxiety, they kept their eyes on the court-house or on the thicket of gloom where their enemies lay. But the woods were as quiet as the pall of shadows over them. Once Rome, making his rounds, saw a figure crawling through a field of corn. It looked like Crump's, but before he could fire the man rolled like a ball down the bushy bank to the river. An instant later some object went swiftly past a side street-somebody on horseback-and a picket fired an alarm. The horse kept on, and Rome threw his rifle on a patch of moonlight, but when the object flashed through, his finger was numbed at the trigger. In the moonlight the horse looked gray, and the rider was seated sidewise. A bullet from the court-house clipped his hat-brim as he ran recklessly across the street to where Steve Marcum stood in the dark behind old Sam's cabin.

"Jim Hale 'll git him as he goes up the road," said Steve, calmly-and then with hot impatience, "Why the hell don't he shoot?

Rome started forward in the moonlight, and Steve caught his arm. Two bullets hissed from the court-house, and he fell back.

A shot sounded from the bushes far away from the road. The horse kept on, and splashed into Troubled Fork, and Steve swore bitterly.

"Hit hain't Jim. Hit's that mis'able Bud Vickers; he's been a-stan din' guard out'n the bushes 'stid o' the road. That was a spy, I tell ye, 'n' the coward let him in and let him out. They'll know now we're all drunk! Whut's the matter?

Rome's mouth was half open. He looked white and sick, and Steve thought he had been hit, but he took off his hat. " Purty close! " he said, with a laugh, pointing at the bullet-hole through the brim.

Steve, unsuspicious, went on: "Hit was a spy, I tell ye. Bud was afeard to stan' in the road, 'n' I'm goin' out thar 'n' twist his damned neck. We've got 'em, Rome! I tell ye, we've got 'em! Ef we kin git through this night, and git the boys sober in the morning, we've got 'em shore!"

The night did pass in safety, darkness wore away without attack, and morning broke on the town in its drunken stupor. Then the curious silence of the Lewallens was explained. The rumor came that old Jasper was dead, and it went broadcast. Later, friends coming to the edge of the town for the bodies of the dead Lewallens confirmed it. A random ball had passed through old Lewallen's body in the wild flight for the woods, and during the night he had spent his last breath in a curse against the man who fired it.

Then each Stetson, waked from his drunken sleep, drank again when he heard of the death. The day bade fair to be like the night, and again the anxiety of the leaders was edged with fear. Old Jasper dead and young Jasper a prisoner, the chance was near to end the feud, or there would be no Lewallen left to lead their enemies. But, again, they were wellnigh helpless. Already they had barely enough men to guard their prisoners. Of the Marcums, Steve alone was able to handle a Winchester, and outside the sounds of the carousal were in the air and growing louder. In a little while, if the Lewallens but knew it, escape would be easy and the Stetsons could be driven from the town.

Oh, they know it," said Steve. "They'll be a-whoopin' down out O' them woods purty soon, 'n' we re goin to ketch hell. I'd like to know mighty well who that spy was last night. That cussed Bud Vickers says it was a ha'nt, on a white hoss, with long hair flyin' in the wind, 'n' that he shot plumb through it. I jus' wish I'd a had a chance at it."

Still, noon came again without trouble, and the imprisoned Lewallens had been twenty-four hours without food. Their ammunition was getting scarce. The firing was less frequent, though the watch was as close as ever, and twice a Winchester had sounded a signal of distress. All knew that a response must come soon; and come it did. A picket, watching the river road, saw young Jasper's horse coming along the dark bushes far up the river, and brought the news to the group standing behind old Sam's cabin. The gray galloped into sight, and, skirting the woods, came straight for the town-with a woman on his back. The stirrup of a man's saddle dangled on one side, and the woman's bonnet had fallen from her head. Some one challenged her.

Stop, I tell ye! Don't ye go near that courthouse! Stop, I tell ye! I'll shoot! Stop!"

Rome ran from the cabin with a revolver in each hand. A drunken mountaineer was raising a Winchester to his shoulder, and, springing from the back of the gray at the court-house steps, was Martha Lewallen.

"I'll kill the fust man that lifts his finger to hurt the gal," Rome said, knocking the drunken man's gun in the air. "We hain't fightin' women!"

It was too late to oppose her, and the crowd stood helplessly watching. No one dared approach, so, shielding with her body the space of the opening door, she threw the sack of food within. Then she stood a moment talking and, turning, climbed to her saddle. The gray was spotted with foam, and showed the red of his nostrils with every breath as, with face flushed and eyes straight before her, she rode slowly toward the crowd. What was she about? Rome stood rigid, his forgotten pistols hanging at each side; the mouth of the drunken mountaineer was open with stupid wonder; the rest fell apart as she came around the corner of the cabin and, through the space given, rode slowly, her skirt almost brushing Rome, looking neither to the right nor to the left; and when she had gone quite through them all, she wheeled and rode, still slowly, through the open fields toward the woods which sheltered the Lewallens, while the crowd stood in bewildered silence looking after her. Yells of laughter came from the old court-house. Some of the Stetsons laughed, too; some swore, a few grumbled; but there was not one who was not stirred by the superb daring of the girl, though she had used it only to show her contempt.

" Rome, you're a fool; though, fer a fac', we can't shoot a woman; 'n' anyways I ruther shoot her than the hoss. But lemme tell ye, thar was more'n sump'n to eat in that bag! They air up to some dodge."

Rufe Stetson had watched the incident through a port-hole of the cabin, and his tone was at once jesting and anxious.

"That grub won't last more'n one day, I reckon," said the drunken mountaineer. We'll watch out fer the gal nex' time. We're boun' to git 'em one time or t'other."

"She rid through us to find out how many of us wasn't dead drunk," said Steve Marcum, still watching the girl as she rode on, toward the woods; "'n' I'm a-thinkin' they'll be down on us purty soon now, 'n' I reckon we'll have to run fer it. Look thar boys!"

The girl had stopped at the edge of the woods; facing the town, she waved her bonnet high above her head.

"Well, whut in the—! "he said, with slow emphasis, and then he leaped from the door with a yell. The bonnet was a signal to the beleaguered Lewallens. The rear door of the courthouse had been quietly opened, and the prisoners were out in a body and scrambling over the fence before the pickets could give an alarm. The sudden yells, the crack of Winchesters, startled even the revellers and all who could, headed by Rome and Steve Marcum, sprang into the square, and started in pursuit. But the Lewallens had got far ahead, and were running in zigzag lines to dodge the balls flying after them. Half-way to the woods was a gully of red clay, and into this the fleetest leaped, and turned instantly to cover their comrades. The Winchesters began to rattle from the woods, and the bullets came like rain from everywhere.

"T-h-up! T-h-up! T-h-up! " there were three of them-the peculiar soft, dull messages of hot lead to living flesh. A Stetson went down; another stumbled; Rufe Stetson, climbing the fence, caught at his breast with an oath, and fell back. Rome and Steve dropped for safety to the ground. Every other Stetson turned in a panic, and every Lewallen in the gully leaped from it, and ran under the Lewallen fire for shelter in the woods. The escape was over.

"That was a purty neat trick," said Steve, wiping a red streak from his cheek. " Nex' time she tries that, she'll git herself into trouble."

At nightfall the wounded leader and the dead one were carried up the mountain, each to his home; and there was mourning far into the night on one bank of the Cumberland, and, serious though Rufe Stetson's wound was, exultation on the other. But in it Rome could take but little part. There had been no fault to find with him in the fight. But a reaction had set in when he saw the girl flash in the moonlight past the sights of his Winchester, and her face that day had again loosed within him a flood of feeling that drove the lust for revenge from his veins. Even now, while he sat in his own cabin, his thoughts were across the river where Martha, broken at last, sat at her death vigils. He knew what her daring ride that day had cost her, with old Jasper dead out there in the woods; and as she passed him he had grown suddenly humbled, shamed. He grew heart-sick now as he thought of it all; and the sight of his mother on her bed in the corner, close to death as she was, filled him with bitterness. There was no help for him. He was alone now, pitted against young Jasper alone. On one bed lay his uncle-nigh to death. There was the grim figure in the corner, the implacable spirit of hate and revenge. His rifle was against the wall. If there was any joy for him in old Jasper's death, it was that his hand had not caused it, and yet-God help him!-there was the other cross, the other oath.

XII

THE star and the crescent were swinging above Wolf's Head, and in the dark hour that breaks into dawn a cavalcade of Lewallens forded the Cumberland, and galloped along the Stetson shore. At the head rode young Jasper, and Crump the spy.

Swift changes had followed the court-house fight. In spite of the death of Rufe Stetson from his wound, and several other Stetsons from ambush, the Lewallens had lost ground. Old Jasper's store had fallen into the hands of creditors -" furriners "-for debts, and it was said his homestead must follow. In a private war a leader must be more than leader. He must feed and often clothe his followers, and young Jasper had not the means to carry on the feud. The famine had made corn dear. He could feed neither man nor horse, and the hired feudsmen fell away, leaving the Lewallens and the Braytons and their close kin to battle alone. So Jasper avoided open combat and resorted to ambush and surprise; and, knowing in some way every move made by the Stetsons, with great daring and success. It was whispered, too, that he no longer cared who owned what he might want for himself. Several dark deeds were traced to him. In a little while he was a terror to good citizens, and finally old Gabe asked aid of the Governor. Soldiers from the settlements were looked for any day, and both factions knew it. At the least this would delay the war, and young Jasper had got ready for a last fight, which was close at hand.

Half a mile on the riders swerved into a wooded slope. There they hid their horses in the brush, and climbed the spur stealthily. The naked woods showed the cup-like shape of the mountains there-a basin from which radiated upward wooded ravines, edged with ribs of rock. In this basin the Stetsons were encamped. The smoke of a fire was visible in the dim morning light, and the Lewallens scattered to surround the camp, but the effort was vain. A picket saw the creeping figures;

his gun echoed a warning from rock to rock, and with yells the Lewallens ran forward. Rome sprang from his sleep near the fire, bareheaded, rifle in hand, his body plain against a huge rock, and the bullets hissed and spat about him as he leaped this way and that, firing as he sprang, and shouting for his men. Steve Marcum alone answered. Some, startled from sleep, had fled in a panic; some had run deeper into the woods for shelter. And bidding Steve save himself, Rome turned up the mountain, running from tree to tree, and dropped unhurt behind a fallen chestnut. Other Stetsons, too, had turned, and answering bullets began to whistle to the enemy, but they were widely separated and ignorant of one another's position, and the Lewallens drove them one by one to new hiding-places, scattering them more. To his right Rome saw Steve Marcum speed like a shadow up through a little open space, but he feared to move, for several Lewallens had recognized him, and were watching him alone. He could not even fire; at the least exposure there was a chorus of bullets about his ears. In a moment they began to come obliquely from each side-the Lewallens were getting around him. In a moment more death was sure there, and once again he darted up the mountain. The bullets sang after him like maddened bees. He felt one cut his hat and another sting his left arm, but he raced up, up, till the firing grew fainter as he climbed, and ceased an instant altogether. Then, still farther below, came a sudden crash of reports. Stetsons were pursuing the men who were after him, but he could not join them. The Lewallens were scattered everywhere between him and his own man, and a descent might lead him to the muzzle of an enemy's Winchester. So he climbed over a ledge of rock and lay there, peeping through a crevice between two bowlders, gaining his breath. The firing was far below him now, and was sharp. Evidently his pursuers were too busy defending themselves to think further of him, and he began to plan how he should get back to his friends. But he kept hidden, and, searching the cliffs below him for a sheltered descent, he saw something like a slouched hat just over a log, scarcely fifty feet below him. Presently the hat was lifted a few inches; a figure rose cautiously and climbed toward the ledge, shielding itself behind rock and tree. Very quietly Rome crawled back to the face of the cliff behind him, and crouched behind a rock with his cocked rifle across his knees. The man must climb over the ledge; there would be a bare, level floor of rock between them-the Lewallen would be at his mercy-and Rome, with straining eyes, waited. There was a footfall on the other side of the ledge; a soft clink of metal against stone. The Lewallen was climbing slowly-slowly. Rome could hear his heavy breathing. A grimy hand slipped over the sharp comb of the ledge; another appeared, clinched about a Winchester-then the slouched hat, and under it the dark, crafty face of young Jasper. Rome sat like the stone before him, with a half-smile on his lips. Jasper peered about with the sly caution of a fox, and his face grew puzzled and chagrined as he looked at the cliffs above him.

"Stop thar!"

He was drawing himself over the ledge, and the low, stern voice startled him, as a knife might have done, thrust suddenly from the empty air at his breast. Rome rose upright against the cliff, with his resolute face against the stock of a Winchester.

"Drap that gun!"

The order was given along Stetson's barrel, and the weapon was dropped, the steel ringing on the stone floor. Rome lowered his gun to the hollow of his arm, and the two young leaders faced each other for the first time in the life of either.

Seem kinder s'prised to see me," said the Stetson, grimly. " Hev ye got a pistol?

Young Jasper glared at him in helpless ferocity.

"Naw!"

"Knife?"

He drew a long-bladed penknife from his pocket, and tossed it at Rome's feet.

"Jes' move over thar, will ye?"

The Lewallen took his stand against the cliff. Rome picked up the fallen rifle and leaned it against the ledge.

"Now, Jas Lewallen, thar's nobody left in this leetle trouble 'cept you 'n' me, 'n' ef one of us was dead, I reckon t'other could live hyeh, 'n' thar'd be peace in these mount'ins. I thought o' that when I had ye at the eend o' this Winchester. I reckon you would 'a' shot me dead ef I had poked my head over a rock as keerless as you." That is just what he would have done, and Jasper did not answer. "I've swore to kill ye, too," added Rome, tapping his gun; "I've got a cross fer ye hyeh."

The Lewallen was no coward. Outcry or resistance was useless. The Stetson meant to taunt him, to make death more bitter; for Jasper expected death, and he sullenly waited for it against the cliff.

"You've been banterin me a long time now, 'lowin' as how ye air the better man o' the two; n' I've got a notion o' givin' ye a chance to prove yer tall talk. Hit's not our way to kill a man in cold blood, 'n' I don't want to kill ye anyways ef I kin he'p it. Seem s'prised ag'in. Reckon ye don't believe me? I don't wonder when I think o' my own dad, 'n' all the meanness yo folks have done mine; but I've got a good reason fer not killin' ye-ef I kin he'p it. Y'u don't know what it is, 'n' y'u'll never know; but I'll give yer a chance now fer yer life ef y'u'll sw'ar on a stack o' Bibles as high as that tree thar that y'u'll leave these mount'ins ef I whoops ye, 'n' nuver come back ag'in as long as you live. I'll leave, ef ye whoops me. Now whut do ye say? Will ye sw'ar?

"I reckon I will, seem' as I've got to," was the surly answer. But Jasper's face was dark with suspicion, and Rome studied it keenly. The Lewallens once had been men whose word was good, but he did not like Jasper's look.

"I reckon I'll trust ye," he said, at last, more through confidence in his own strength than faith in his enemy; foi Jasper whipped would be as much at his mercy as he was now. So Rome threw off his coat, and began winding his homespun suspenders about his waist. Watching him closely, Jasper did the same.

The firing below had ceased. A flock of mountain vultures were sailing in great circles over the thick woods. Two eagles swept straight from the rim of the sun above Wolf's Head, beating over a turbulent sea of mist for the cliffs, scarcely fifty yards above the ledge, where a pine-tree grew between two rocks. At the instant of lighting, they wheeled away, each with a warning scream to the other. A figure lying flat behind the pine had frightened them, and now a face peeped to one side, flushed with eagerness over the coming fight. Both were ready now, and the Lewallen grew suddenly white as Rome turned again and reached down for the guns.

"I reckon I'll put 'em a leetle furder out o' the way," he said, kicking the knife over the cliff; and, standing on a stone, he thrust them into a crevice high above his head.

"Now, Jas, we'll fight this gredge out, as our grandads have done afore us."

Lewallen and Stetson were man to man at last. Suspicion was gone now, and a short, brutal laugh came from the cliff.

"I'll fight ye! Oh, by God, I'll fight ye!"

The ring of the voice struck an answering gleam from Rome's gray eyes, and the two sprang for each other. It was like the struggle of primeval men who had not yet learned even the use of clubs. For an instant both stood close, like two wild beasts crouched for a spring, and circling about to get at each other's throats, with mouths set, eyes watching eyes, and hands twitching nervously. Young Jasper leaped first, and the Stetson, wary of closing with him, shrank back. There were a few quick, heavy blows, and the Lewallen was beaten away with blood at his lips. Then each knew the advantage of the other. The Stetson's reach was longer; the Lewallen was shorter and heavier, and again he closed in. Again Rome sent out his long arm. A turn of Jasper's head let the heavy fist pass over his shoulder. The force of the blow drove Rome forward; the two clinched, and Jasper's arms tightened about the Stetson's waist. With a quick gasp for breath Rome loosed his hold, and, bending his enemy's head back with one hand, rained blow after blow in his face with the other. One terrible stroke on the jaw, and Jasper's arms were loosed; the two fell apart, the one stunned, the other breathless. One dazed moment only, and for a third time the Lewallen came on. Rome had been fighting a man; now he faced a demon. Jasper's brows stood out like bristles, and the eyes under them were red and fierce like a mad bull's. Again Rome's blows fell, but again the Lewallen reached him, and this time he got his face under the Stetson's chin, -'id the heavy fist fell upon the back of his head, and upon his neck, as upon wood and leather. Again Rome had to gasp for breath, and again the two were fiercely locked-their corded arms as tense as serpents. Around and around they whirled, straining, tripping, breaking the silence only with deep, quick breaths and the stamping of feet, Jasper firm on the rock, and Rome's agility saving him from being lifted in the air and tossed from the cliff. There was no pause for rest. It was a struggle to the end, and a quick one; and under stress of excitement the figure at the pine-tree had risen to his knees- jumping even to his feet in plain view, when the short, strong arms of the Lewallen began at last to draw Rome closer still, and to bend him backward. The Stetson was giving way at last. The Lewallen's vindictive face grew blacker, and his white teeth showed between his snarling lips as he fastened one leg behind his enemy's, and, with chin against his shoulder, bent him slowly, slowly back. The two breathed in short, painful gasps; their swollen muscles trembled under the strain as with ague. Back - back - the Stetson was falling; he seemed almost down, when-the trick is an old one-whirling with the quickness of light, he fell heavily on his opponent, and caught him by the throat with both hands.

"'Nough? " he asked, hoarsely. It was the first word uttered.

The only answer was a fierce struggle. Rome felt the Lewallen's teeth sinking in his arm, and his fingers tightened like twisting steel, till Jasper caught his breath as though strangling to death.

"'Nough?" asked the hoarse voice again.

No answer; tighter clinched the fingers. The Lewallen shook his head feebly; his purple face paled suddenly as Rome loosed his hold, and his lips moved in a whisper.

"'Nough!"

Rome rose dizzily to one knee. Jasper turned, gasping, and lay with his face to the rock. For a while both were quiet, Rome, panting with open mouth and white with exhaustion, looking down now and then at the Lewallen, whose face was turned away with shame.

The sun was blazing above Wolf's Head now, and the stillness about them lay unbroken on the woods below.

"I've whooped ye, Jas," Rome said, at last; "I've whooped ye in a fa'r fight, 'n' I've got nothin' now to say 'bout yer tall talk, 'n' I reckon you hevn't nuther. Now, hit's understood, hain't it, that y'u'll leave these mount'ins?

Y'u kin go West," he continued, as the Lewallen did not answer. " Uncle Rufe used to say thar's a good deal to do out thar, 'n' nobody axes questions. Thar's no-body left hyeh but you 'n' me, but these mount'ins was never big 'nough fer one Lewallen 'n' one Stetson, 'n' you've got to go. I reckon ye won't believe me, but I'm glad I didn't hev to kill ye. But you've promised to go, now, 'n' I'll take yer word fer it." He turned his face, and the Lewallen, knowing it from the sound of his voice, sprang to his feet.

"Oh-!"

A wild curse burst from Rome's lips, and both leaped for the guns. The Lewallen had the start of a few feet, and Rome, lamed in the fight, stumbled and fell. Before he could rise Jasper had whirled, with one of the Winchesters above his head and his face aflame with fury. Asking no mercy, Rome hid his face with one arm and waited, stricken faint all at once, and numb. One report struck his ears, muffled, whip-like. A dull wonder came to him that the Lewallen could have missed at such close range, and he waited for another. Some one shouted-a shrill hallo. A loud laugh followed; a light seemed breaking before Rome's eyes, and he lifted his head. Jasper was on his face again, motionless; and Steve Marcum's tall figure was climbing over a bowlder toward him.

"That was the best fight I've seed in my time, by God," he said, coolly, " 'n', Rome, y'u air the biggest fool this side o' the settlements, I reckon. I had dead aim on him, 'n' I was jest a-thinkin' hit was a purty good thing fer you that old long-nosed Jim Stover chased me up hyeh, when, damn me, ef that boy up thar didn't let his ole gun loose. I'd a-got Jas myself ef he hadn't been so all-fired quick o' trigger."

Up at the root of the pine-tree Isom stood motionless, with his long rifle in one hand and a little cloud of smoke breaking above his white face. When Rome looked up he started down without a word. Steve swung himself over the ledge.

"I heerd the shootin'," said the boy, " up thar at the cave, 'n' I couldn't stay thar. I knowed ye could whoop him, Rome, 'n' I seed Steve, too, but I was afeard-" Then he saw the body. His tongue stopped, his face shrivelled, and Steve, hanging with one hand to the ledge, watched him curiously.

" Rome," said the boy, in a quick whisper, "is he daid?"

" Come on! " said Steve, roughly. "They'll be up hyeh atter us in a minute. Leave Jas's gun thar, 'n' send that boy back home."

That day the troops came-young Blue Grass Kentuckians. That night, within the circle of their camp-fires, a last defiance was cast in the teeth of law and order. Flames rose within the old court- house, and before midnight the moonlight fell on four black walls. That night, too, the news of young Jasper's fate was carried to the death-bed of Rome's mother, and before day the old woman passed in peace. That day Stetsons and Lewallens disbanded. The Lewallens had no leader; the Stetsons, no enemies to fight. Some hid, some left the mountains, some gave themselves up for trial. Upon Rome Stetson the burden fell. Against him the law was set. A price was put on his head, his house was burned-a last act of Lewallen hate-and Rome was homeless, the last of his race, and an outlaw.

XIII

WITH the start of a few hours and the sympathy of his people one mountaineer can defy the army of the United States; and the mountaineers usually laugh when they hear troops are coming. For the time they stop fighting and hide in the woods; and when the soldiers are gone, they come out again, and begin anew their little pleasantries. But the soldiers can protect the judge on his bench and the county-seat in time of court, and for these purposes they serve well.

The search for Rome Stetson, then, was useless. His friends would aid him; his enemies feared to betray him. So the soldiers marched away one morning, and took their prisoners for safe- keeping in the Blue Grass, until court should open at Hazlan.

Meantime, spring came and deepened-the mountain spring. The berries of the wintergreen grew scarce, and Rome Stetson, " hiding out," as the phrase is, had to seek them on thc northem face of the mountains. The moss on the naked winter trees brightened in color, and along the river, where willows drooped, ran faint lines of green. The trailing arbutus gave out delicate pink blossoms, and the south wind blew apart the petals of the anemone. Soon violets unfolded above the dead leaves; azaleas swung their yellow trumpets through the undergrowth; over-head, the dogwood tossed its snow-flakes in gusts through the green and gold of new leaves and sunlight; and higher still waved the poplar blooms, with honey ready on every crimson heart for the bees. Down in the valley Rome Stetson could see about every little cabin pink clouds and white clouds of peach and of apple blossoms. Amid the ferns about him shade-loving trilliums showed their many-hued faces, and every opening was thickly peopled with larkspur seeking the sun. The giant magnolia and the umbrella-tree spread their great creamy flowers; the laurel shook out myriads of pink and white bells, and the queen of mountain flowers was stirring from sleep in the buds of the rhododendron.

With the spring new forces pulsed the mountain air. The spirit of the times reached even Hazlan. A railroad was coming up the river, so the rumor was. When winter broke, surveyors had appeared; after them, mining experts and purchasers of land. New ways of bread-making were open to all, and the feudsman began to see that he could make food and clothes more easily and with less danger than by sleeping with his rifle in the woods, and by fighting men who had done him no harm. Many were tired of fighting; many, forced into the feud, had fought unwillingly. Others had sold their farms and wild lands, and were moving toward the Blue Grass or westward. The desperadoes of each faction had fled the law or were in its clutches. The last Lewallen was dead; the last Stetson was hidden away in the mountains. There were left Mareums and Braytons, but only those who felt safest from indictment; in these a spirit of hostility would live for years, and, roused by passion or by drink, would do murder now on one side of the Cumberland and now on the other; but the Stetson-Lewallen feud, old Gabe believed, was at an end at last.

All these things the miller told Rome Stetson, who well knew what they meant. He was safe enough from the law while the people took no part in his capture, but he grew apprehensive when he learned of the changes going on in the valley. None but old Gabe knew where he was, to be sure, but with his own enemies to guide the soldiers he could not hope to remain hidden long. Still, with that love of the mountains characteristic of all races born among them, he clung to his own land. He would rather stay where he was the space of a year and die, he told old Gabe passionately, than live to old age in another State.

But there was another motive, and he did not hide it. On the other side he had one enemy left-the last, too, of her race-who was more to him than his own dead kindred, who hated him, who placed at his door all her sorrows. For her he was living like a wolf in a cave, and old Gabe knew it. Her-he would not leave.

"I tell ye, Rome, you've got to go. Thar's no use talkin'. Court comes the fust Monday in June. The soldiers ull be hyeh. Hit won't be safe. Thar's some that s'picions I know whar ye air now, 'n' they'll be spyin', 'n' mebbe hit'll git me into trouble, too, aidin' 'n' abettin' a man to git away who air boun' to the law."

The two were sitting on the earthen floor of the cave before a little fire, and

Rome, with his hands about his knees and his brows knitted, was staring into the yellow blaze. His unshorn hair fell to his shoulders; his face was pale from insufficient food and exercise, and tense with a look that was at once caged and defiant.

"Uncle Gabe," he asked, quietly, for the old man's tone was a little querulous, " air ye sorry ye holped me? Do ye blame me fer whut I've done?"

"No," said the old miller, answering both questions; "I don't. I believe whut ye tol' me. Though, even ef ye had 'a' done it, I don't know as I'd blame ye, seem' that it was a fa'r fight. I don't doubt he was doin' his best to kill you."

Rome turned quickly, his face puzzled and darkening.

Uncle Gabe, whut air you drivin' at? " The old man spat into the fire, and shifted his position uneasily, as Rome's hand caught his knee.

Well, ef I have to tell ye, I s'pose I must. Thar's been nothin' pertickler ag'in ye so fer, 'cept fer breakin' that confederatin' statute 'bout bandin' fightin' men together; 'n' nobody was very anxious to git hol' o' ye jes fer that, but now "-the old man stopped a moment, for Rome's eyes were kindling-" they say that ye killed Jas Lew allen, 'n' that ye air a murderer; 'n' hit air powerful strange how all of a suddint folks seem to be gittin' down on a man as kills his fellow-creetur; 'n' now they means to hunt ye til they ketch ye."

It was all out now, and the old man was relieved. Rome rose to his feet, and in sheer agony of spirit paced the floor.

"I tol' ye, Uncle Gabe, that I didn't kill him."

So ye did, 'n' I believe ye. But a feller seed you 'n' Steve comm' from the place whar Jas was found dead, 'n' whar the dirt 'n' rock was throwed about as by two bucks in spring-time. Steve says he didn't do it, 'n' he wouldn't say you didn't. Looks to me like Steve did the kuhn', 'n' was lyin' a leetle. He hain't goin' to confess hit to save your neck; 'n' he can't no way, fer he hev lit out o' these mount'ins-long ago."

If Steve was out of danger, suspicion could not harm him, and Rome said nothing.

"Isom's got the lingerin' fever ag'in, 'n' he's out"i his head. He's ravin' 'bout that fight. Looks like ye tol' him 'bout it. He says,' Don't tell Uncle Gabe'; 'n' he keeps sayin' it. Hit'll 'most kill him ef you go 'way; but he wants ye to git out o' the mount'ins; 'n', Rome, you've got to go."

"Who was it, Uncle Gabe, that seed me 'n' Steve comm' 'way from thar?

He air the same feller who hev been spyin' ye all the time this war's been goin' on; hit's that dried-faced, snaky Eli Crump, who ye knocked down 'n' choked up in Hazlan one day fer sayin' something ag'in Isom."

"I knowed it-I knowed it-oh, ef I could git my fingers roun' his throat once more-jes once more-I'd be 'mos' ready to die."

He stretched out his hands as he strode back and forth, with his fingers crooked like talons; his shadow leaped from wall to wall, and his voice, filling the cave, was, for the moment, scarcely human. The old man waited till the paroxysm was over and Rome had again sunk before the fire.

"Hit 'u'd do no good, Rome," he said, rising to go. "You've got enough on ye now, without the sin o' takin' his life. You better make up yer mind to leave the mount ins now right 'way. You're a-gittin' no more'n half-human, livin' up hyeh like a catamount. I don't see how ye kin stand it. Thar's no hope o' things blowin' over, boy, 'n' givin' ye a chance o' comm' out ag'in, as yer dad and yer grandad usen to do afore ye. The citizens air gittin' tired o' these wars. They keeps out the fur-riners who makes roads 'n' buys lands; they air ag'in' the law, ag'in' religion, ag'in' yo' pocket, 'n' ag'in' mine. Lots o' folks hev been ag'in' all this fightin' fer a long time, but they was too skeery to say so. They air talkin' mighty big now, seem' they kin git soldiers hyeh to pertect 'em. So ye mought as well give up the idea o' staying hyeh, 'less'n ye want to give yourself up to the law."

The two stepped from the cave, and passed through the rhododendrons till they stood on the cliff overlooking the valley. The rich light lay like a golden mist between the mountains, and through it, far down, the river moaned like the wind of a coming storm.

Did ye tell the gal whut I tol' ye?"

"Yes, Rome; hit wasn't no use. She says Steve's word's as good as yourn; 'n' she knowed about the crosses. Folks say she swore awful ag'in' ye at young Jas's burial, 'lowin' that she'd hunt ye down herse'f, ef the soldiers didn't ketch ye. I hain't seed her sence she got sick; 'pears like ever'body's sick. Mebbe she's a leetle settled down now-no tellin'. No use foolin' with her, Rome. You git away from hyeh. Don't you worry 'bout Isom-I'll take keer o' him, 'n' when he gits well, he'll want to come at-ter ye, 'n' I'll let him go. He couldn't live hyeh without you. But y'u must git away,

Rome, 'n' git away mighty quick."

With hands clasped behind him, Rome stood and watched the bent figure slowly pick its way around the stony cliff.

"I reckon I've got to go. She's ag'in' me; they're all ag'in' me. I reckon I've jes got to go. Somehow, I've been kinder hopin'-" He closed his lips to check the groan that rose to them, and turned again into the gloom behind him.

XIV

JUNE came. The wild rose swayed above its image along every little shadowed stream, and the scent of wild grapes was sweet in the air and as vagrant as a bluebird's note in autumn. The rhododendrons burst into beauty, making gray ridge and gray cliff blossom with purple, hedging streams with snowy clusters and shining leaves, and lighting up dark coverts in the woods as with white stars. The leaves were full, woodthrushes sang, and bees droned like unseen running water in the woods.

With June came circuit court once more-and the soldiers. Faint music pierced the dreamy chant of the river one morning as Rome lay on a bowlder in the summer sun; and he watched the guns flashing like another stream along the water, and then looked again to the Lewallen cabin. Never, morning, noon, or night, when he came from the rhododendrons, or when they closed about him, did he fail to turn his eyes that way. Often he would see a bright speck moving about the dim lines of the cabin, and he would scarcely breathe while he watched it, so easily would it disappear. Always he had thought it was Martha, and now he knew it was, for the old miller had told him more of the girl, and had wrung his heart with pity. She had been ill a long while. The "furriners " had seized old Jasper's cahin and land. The girl was homeless, and she did not know it, for no one had the heart to tell her. She was living with the Braytons; and every day she went to the cabin, "moonin" n' sorrowin' aroun'," as old Gabe said; and she was much changed.

Once more the miller came-for the last time, he said, firmly. Crump had trailed him, and had learned where Rome was. The search would begin next day-perhaps that very night-and Crump would guide the soldiers. Now he must go, and go quickly. The boy, too, sent word that unless Rome went, he would have something to tell. Old Gabe saw no significance in the message; but he had promised to deliver it, and he did. Rome wavered then; Steve and himself gone, no suspicion would fall on the lad. If he were caught, the boy might confess. With silence Rome gave assent, and the two parted in an apathy that was like heartlessness. Only old Gabe's shrunken breast heaved with something more than weariness of descent, and Rome stood watching him a long time before he turned back to the cave that had sheltered him from his enemies among beasts and men. In a moment he came out for the last time, and turned the opposite way. Climbing about the spur, he made for the path that led down to the river. When he reached it he glanced at the sun, and stopped in indecision. Straight above him was a knoll, massed with rhodo-dendrons, the flashing leaves of which made it like a great sea-wave in the slanting sun, while the blooms broke slowly down over it like foam. Above this was a gray sepulchre of dead, standing trees, more gaunt and spectre-like than ever, with the rich life of summer about it. Higher still were a dark belt of stunted firs and the sandstone ledge, and above these-home. He was risking his liberty, his life. Any clump of bushes might bristle suddenly with Winchesters. If the soldiers sought for him at the cave they would at the same time guard the mountain paths; they would guard, too, the Stetson cabin. But no matter-the sun was still high, and he turned up the steep. The ledge passed, he stopped with a curse at his lips and the pain of a knife-thrust at his heart. A heap of blackened stones and ashes was before him. The wild mountain-grass was growing up about it. The bee-gums were overturned and rifled. The garden was a tangled mass of weeds. The graves in the little family burying-ground were unprotected, the fence was gone, and no boards marked the last two ragged mounds. Old Gabe had never told him. He, too, like Martha, was homeless, and the old miller had been kind to him, as the girl's kinspeople had been to her.

For a long while he sat on the remnant of the burned and broken fence, and once more the old tide of bitterness rose within him and ebbed away. There were none left to hate, to wreak vengeance on. It was hard to leave the ruins as they were; and yet he would rather leave weeds and ashes than, like Martha, have some day to know that his home was in the hands of a stranger. When he thought of the girl he grew calmer; his own sorrows gave way to the thought of hers; and half from habit he raised his face to look across the river. Two eagles swept from a dark ravine under the shelf of rock where he had fought young Jasper, and made for a sun-lighted peak on the other shore. From them his gaze fell to Wolf's Head and to the cabin beneath, and a name passed his lips in a whisper.

Then he took the path to the river, and he found the canoe where old Gabe had hidden it. Before the young moon rose he pushed into the stream and drifted with the current. At the mouth of the creek that ran over old Gabe's water-wheel he turned the prow to the Lewallen shore.

Not yit! Not yit! " he said.

XV

THAT night Rome passed in the woods, with his rifle, in a bed of leaves. Before daybreak he had built a fire in a deep ravine to cook his breakfast, and had scattered the embers that the smoke should give no sign. The sun was high when he crept cautiously in sight of the Lewallen cabin. It was much like his own home on the other shore, except that the house, closed and desolate, was standing, and the bees were busy. At the corner of the kitchen a rusty axe was sticking in a half-cut piece of timber, and on the porch was a heap of kindling and fire wood-the last work old Jasper and his son had ever done. In the Lewallens' garden, also, two graves were fresh; and the spirit of neglect and ruin overhung the place.

All the morning he waited in the edge of the laurel, peering down the path, watching the clouds race with their shadows over the mountains, or pacing to and fro in his covert of leaves and flowers. He began to fear at last that she was not coming, that she was ill, and once he started down the mountain toward Steve Brayton's cabin. The swift descent brought him to his senses, and he stopped half-way, and climbed back again to his hiding-place. What he was doing, what he meant to do, he hardly knew. Mid-day passed; the sun fell toward the mountains, and once more came the fierce impulse to see her, even though he must stalk into the Brayton cabin. Again, half-crazed, he started impetuously through the brush, and shrank back, and stood quiet. A little noise down the path had reached his ear. In a moment he could hear slow foot-falls, and the figure of the girl parted the pink-and-white laurel blossoms, which fell in a shower about her when she brushed through them. She passed quite near him, walking slowly, and stopped for a moment to rest against a pillar of the porch. She was very pale; her face was traced deep with suffering, and she was, as old Gabe said, much changed. Then she went on toward the garden, stepping with an effort over the low fence, and leaned as if weak and tired against the apple-tree, the boughs of which shaded the two graves at her feet. For a few moments she stood there, listless, and Rome watched her with hungry eyes, at a loss what to do. She moved presently, and walked quite around the graves without looking at them; then came back past him, and, seating herself in the porch, turned her face to the river. The sun lighted her hair, and in the sunken, upturned eyes Rome saw the shimmer of tears.

"Marthy! " He couldn't help it-the thick, low cry broke like a groan from his lips, and the girl was on her feet, facing him. She did not know the voice, nor the shaggy, half-wild figure in the shade of the laurel; and she started back as if to run; but seeing that the man did not mean to harm her, she stopped, looking for a moment with wonder and even with quick pity at the hunted face with its white appeal. Then a sudden spasm caught her throat, and left her body rigid, her hands shut, and her eyes dry and hard-she knew him. A slow pallor drove the flush of surprise from her face, and her lips moved once, but there was not even a whisper from them. Rome raised one hand before his face, as though to ward off something. " Don't look at mc that way, Marthy-my God, don't! I didn't kill him. I sw'ar it! I give him a chance fer his life. I know, I know-Steve says he didn't. Thar was only us two. Hit looks ag'in' me; but I hain't killed one nur t'other. I let 'em both go. Y'u don't believe me? " He went swiftly toward her, his gun outstretched. Hyeh, gal! I heerd ye swore ag' in' me out thar in the gyarden-'lowin' that you was goin' to hunt me down yerself if the soldiers didn't. Hyeh's yer chance!

The girl shrank away from him, too startled to take the weapon; and he leaned it against her, and stood away, with his hands behind him.

Kill me ef ye think I'm a-lyin' to ye," he said. "Y'u kin git even with me now. But I want to tell ye fust "-the girl had caught the muzzle of the gun convulsively, and was bending over it, her eyes burning, her face inscrutable-hit was a fa'r fight betwixt us, 'n' I whooped him. He got his gun then, 'n' would 'a' killed me ag'in' his oath ef he hadn't been shot fust Hit's so, too, 'bout the crosses. I made 'em; they're right thar on that gun; but whut could I do with mam a-standin' right thar with the gun 'n' Uncle Rufe a-tellin' 'bout my own dad layin' in his blood, 'n' Isom 'n' the boys lookin' on! But I went ag'in' my oath; I gave him his life when I had the right to take it. I could 'a' killed yer dad once, 'n' I had the right to kill him, too, fer killin' mine; but I let him go, 'n' I reckon I done that fer ye, too. 'Pears like I hain't done nothin' sence I seed ye over thar in the mill that day that wasn't done fer ye. Somehow ye put me dead ag'in' my own kin, 'n' tuk away all my hate ag'in' yourn. I couldn't fight fer thinkin' I was fightin' you, 'n' when I seed ye comm' through the bushes jes now, so white 'n' sickly-like, I couldn't hardly git breath, a-thinkin' I was the cause of all yer misery. That's all!" He stretched out his arms. Shoot, gal, ef ye don't believe me. I'd jes as lieve die, ef ye thinks I'm lyin' to ye, 'n' ef ye hates me fer whut I hain't done."

The gun had fallen to the earth. The girl, trembling at the knees, sank to her seat on the porch, and, folding her arms against the pillar, pressed her forehead against them, her face unseen. Rome stooped to pick up the weapon.

"I'm goin' 'way now," he went on, slowly, after a little pause, "but I couldn't leave hyeh without seem' you. I wanted ye to know the truth, 'n' I 'lowed y'u'd believe me ef I tol' ye myself. I've been a-waitin' thar in the lorrel fer ye since mornin'. Uncle Gabe tol' me ye come hyeh ever' day. He says I've got to go. I've been hopin' I mought come out o' the bushes some day. But Uncle Gabe says ever'body's ag'in' me more' n ever, 'n' that the soldiers mean to ketch me. The gov'ner out thar in the settlements says as how he'll give five hundred dollars fer me, livin' or dead. He'll nuver git me livin'-I've swore that-'n' as I hev done nothin' sech as folks on both sides hev done who air walkin' roun' free, I hain't goin' to give up. Hit's purty hard to leave these mount'ins. Reckon I'll nuver see 'em ag'in. Been livin' like a catamount over thar on the knob. I could jes see you over hyeh, 'n' I reckon I hain't done much 'cept lay over thar on a rock 'n' watch ye movin' round. Hit's mighty good to feel that ye believe me, 'n' I want ye to know that I been stayin' over thar fer nothin' on earth but jes to see you ag'in; 'n' I want ye to know that I was a-sorrowin' fer ye when y'u was sick, 'n' a-pinin' to see ye, 'n' a-hopin' some day y'u mought kinder git over yer hate fer me." He had been talking with low tenderness, half to himself, and with his face to the river, and he did not see the girl's tears falling to the porch. Her sorrow gave way in a great sob now, and he turned with sharp remorse, and stood quite near her.

"Don't cry, Marthy," he said. "God knows hit's hard to think I've brought all this on ye when I'd give all these mount 'ins to save ye from it. Whut d' ye say? Don't cry."

The girl was trying to speak at last, and Rome bent over to catch the words.

"I hain't cryin' fer myself," she said, faintly, and then she said no more; but the first smile that had passed over Rome's face for many a day passed then, and he put out one big hand, and let it rest on the heap of lustrous hair.

"Marthy, I hate to go 'way, leavin' ye hyeh with nobody to take keer o' ye. You're all alone hyeh in the mount'ins; I'm all alone; 'n' I reckon I'll be all alone wharever I go, ef you stay hyeh. I got a boat down thar on the river, 'n' I'm goin' out West whar Uncle Rufe use to live. I know I hain't good fer nothin' much "-he spoke almost huskily; he could scarcely get the words to his lips-" but I want ye to go with me. Won't ye?"

The girl did not answer, but her sobbing ceased slowly, while Rome stroked her hair; and at last she lifted her face, and for a moment looked to the other shore. Then she rose. There is a strange pride in the Kentucky mountaineer.

"As you say, Rome, thar's nobody left but you, 'n' nobody but me; but they burned you out, we hain't even-yit." Her eyes were on Thunderstruck Knob, where the last sunlight used to touch the Stetson cabin.

"Hyeh, Rome!" He knew what she meant, and he kneeled at the pile of kindling-wood near the kitchen door. Then they stood back and waited. The sun dipped below a gap in the mountains, the sky darkened, and the flames rose to the shingled porch, and leaped into the gathering dusk. On the outer edge of the quivering light, where it touched the blossomed laurel, the two stood till the blaze caught the eaves of the cabin; and then they turned their faces where, burning to ashes in the west, was another fire, whose light blended in the eyes of each with a light older and more lasting than its own-the light eternal.

THE END

The Codes Of Hammurabi And Moses
W. W. Davies

QTY

The discovery of the Hammurabi Code is one of the greatest achievements of archaeology, and is of paramount interest, not only to the student of the Bible, but also to all those interested in ancient history...

Religion   **ISBN:** *1-59462-338-4*   **Pages:132**
MSRP $12.95

The Theory of Moral Sentiments
Adam Smith

QTY

This work from 1749. contains original theories of conscience amd moral judgment and it is the foundation for systemof morals.

Philosophy   **ISBN:** *1-59462-777-0*   **Pages:536**
MSRP $19.95

Jessica's First Prayer
Hesba Stretton

QTY

In a screened and secluded corner of one of the many railway-bridges which span the streets of London there could be seen a few years ago, from five o'clock every morning until half past eight, a tidily set-out coffee-stall, consisting of a trestle and board, upon which stood two large tin cans, with a small fire of charcoal burning under each so as to keep the coffee boiling during the early hours of the morning when the work-people were thronging into the city on their way to their daily toil...

Pages:84

Childrens   **ISBN:** *1-59462-373-2*   *MSRP $9.95*

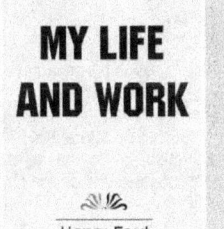

My Life and Work
Henry Ford

QTY

Henry Ford revolutionized the world with his implementation of mass production for the Model T automobile. Gain valuable business insight into his life and work with his own auto-biography... "We have only started on our development of our country we have not as yet, with all our talk of wonderful progress, done more than scratch the surface. The progress has been wonderful enough but..."

Pages:300

Biographies/   **ISBN:** *1-59462-198-5*   *MSRP $21.95*

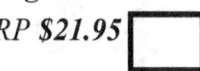

The Art of Cross-Examination
Francis Wellman

QTY

I presume it is the experience of every author, after his first book is published upon an important subject, to be almost overwhelmed with a wealth of ideas and illustrations which could readily have been included in his book, and which to his own mind, at least, seem to make a second edition inevitable. Such certainly was the case with me; and when the first edition had reached its sixth impression in five months, I rejoiced to learn that it seemed to my publishers that the book had met with a sufficiently favorable reception to justify a second and considerably enlarged edition. ...

Pages:412

Reference   **ISBN: *1-59462-647-2***   *MSRP $19.95*

On the Duty of Civil Disobedience
Henry David Thoreau

QTY

Thoreau wrote his famous essay, On the Duty of Civil Disobedience, as a protest against an unjust but popular war and the immoral but popular institution of slave-owning. He did more than write—he declined to pay his taxes, and was hauled off to gaol in consequence. Who can say how much this refusal of his hastened the end of the war and of slavery ?

Law   **ISBN: *1-59462-747-9***   **Pages:48**

MSRP $7.45

Dream Psychology Psychoanalysis for Beginners
Sigmund Freud

QTY

Sigmund Freud, born Sigismund Schlomo Freud (May 6, 1856 - September 23, 1939), was a Jewish-Austrian neurologist and psychiatrist who co-founded the psychoanalytic school of psychology. Freud is best known for his theories of the unconscious mind, especially involving the mechanism of repression; his redefinition of sexual desire as mobile and directed towards a wide variety of objects; and his therapeutic techniques, especially his understanding of transference in the therapeutic relationship and the presumed value of dreams as sources of insight into unconscious desires.

Pages:196

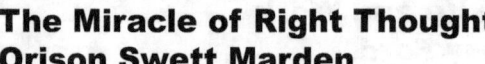

Psychology   **ISBN: *1-59462-905-6***   *MSRP $15.45*

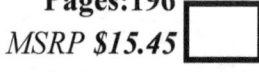

The Miracle of Right Thought
Orison Swett Marden

QTY

Believe with all of your heart that you will do what you were made to do. When the mind has once formed the habit of holding cheerful, happy, prosperous pictures, it will not be easy to form the opposite habit. It does not matter how improbable or how far away this realization may see, or how dark the prospects may be, if we visualize them as best we can, as vividly as possible, hold tenaciously to them and vigorously struggle to attain them, they will gradually become actualized, realized in the life. But a desire, a longing without endeavor, a yearning abandoned or held indifferently will vanish without realization.

Pages:360

Self Help   **ISBN: *1-59462-644-8***   *MSRP $25.45*

The Rosicrucian Cosmo-Conception Mystic Christianity *by Max Heindel*   ISBN: *1-59462-188-8*   **$38.95**
The Rosicrucian Cosmo-conception is not dogmatic, neither does it appeal to any other authority than the reason of the student. It is: not controversial, but is: sent forth in the, hope that it may help to clear..   New Age/Religion Pages 646

Abandonment To Divine Providence *by Jean-Pierre de Caussade*   ISBN: *1-59462-228-0*   **$25.95**
"The Rev. Jean Pierre de Caussade was one of the most remarkable spiritual writers of the Society of Jesus in France in the 18th Century. His death took place at Toulouse in 1751. His works have gone through many editions and have been republished...   Inspirational/Religion Pages 400

Mental Chemistry *by Charles Haanel*   ISBN: *1-59462-192-6*   **$23.95**
Mental Chemistry allows the change of material conditions by combining and appropriately utilizing the power of the mind. Much like applied chemistry creates something new and unique out of careful combinations of chemicals the mastery of mental chemistry...   New Age Pages 354

The Letters of Robert Browning and Elizabeth Barret Barrett 1845-1846 vol II   ISBN: *1-59462-193-4*   **$35.95**
by Robert Browning and Elizabeth Barrett   Biographies Pages 596

Gleanings In Genesis (volume I) *by Arthur W. Pink*   ISBN: *1-59462-130-6*   **$27.45**
Appropriately has Genesis been termed "the seed plot of the Bible" for in it we have, in germ form, almost all of the great doctrines which are afterwards fully developed in the books of Scripture which follow...   Religion/Inspirational Pages 420

The Master Key *by L. W. de Laurence*   ISBN: *1-59462-001-6*   **$30.95**
In no branch of human knowledge has there been a more lively increase of the spirit of research during the past few years than in the study of Psychology, Concentration and Mental Discipline. The requests for authentic lessons in Thought Control, Mental Discipline and...   New Age/Business Pages 422

The Lesser Key Of Solomon Goetia *by L. W. de Laurence*   ISBN: *1-59462-092-X*   **$9.95**
This translation of the first book of the "Lernegton" which is now for the first time made accessible to students of Talismanic Magic was done, after careful collation and edition, from numerous Ancient Manuscripts in Hebrew, Latin, and French...   New Age/Occult Pages 92

Rubaiyat Of Omar Khayyam *by Edward Fitzgerald*   ISBN:*1-59462-332-5*   **$13.95**
Edward Fitzgerald, whom the world has already learned, in spite of his own efforts to remain within the shadow of anonymity, to look upon as one of the rarest poets of the century, was born at Bredfield, in Suffolk, on the 31st of March, 1809. He was the third son of John Purcell...   Music Pages 172

Ancient Law *by Henry Maine*   ISBN: *1-59462-128-4*   **$29.95**
The chief object of the following pages is to indicate some of the earliest ideas of mankind, as they are reflected in Ancient Law, and to point out the relation of those ideas to modern thought.   Religion/History Pages 452

Far-Away Stories *by William J. Locke*   ISBN: *1-59462-129-2*   **$19.45**
"Good wine needs no bush, but a collection of mixed vintages does. And this book is just such a collection. Some of the stories I do not want to remain buried for ever in the museum files of dead magazine-numbers an author's not unpardonable vanity..."   Fiction Pages 272

Life of David Crockett *by David Crockett*   ISBN: *1-59462-250-7*   **$27.45**
"Colonel David Crockett was one of the most remarkable men of the times in which he lived. Born in humble life, but gifted with a strong will, an indomitable courage, and unremitting perseverance..   Biographies/New Age Pages 424

Lip-Reading *by Edward Nitchie*   ISBN: *1-59462-206-X*   **$25.95**
Edward B. Nitchie, founder of the New York School for the Hard of Hearing, now the Nitchie School of Lip-Reading, Inc. wrote "LIP-READING Principles and Practice". The development and perfecting of this meritorious work on lip-reading was an undertaking...   How-to Pages 400

A Handbook of Suggestive Therapeutics, Applied Hypnotism, Psychic Science   ISBN: *1-59462-214-0*   **$24.95**
by Henry Munro   Health/New Age/Health/Self-help Pages 376

A Doll's House: and Two Other Plays *by Henrik Ibsen*   ISBN: *1-59462-112-8*   **$19.95**
Henrik Ibsen created this classic when in revolutionary 1848 Rome. Introducing some striking concepts in playwriting for the realist genre, this play has been studied the world over.   Fiction/Classics/Plays 308

The Light of Asia *by sir Edwin Arnold*   ISBN: *1-59462-204-3*   **$13.95**
In this poetic masterpiece, Edwin Arnold describes the life and teachings of Buddha. The man who was to become known as Buddha to the world was born as Prince Gautama of India but he rejected the worldly riches and abandoned the reigns of power when... Religion/History/Biographies Pages 170

The Complete Works of Guy de Maupassant *by Guy de Maupassant*   ISBN: *1-59462-157-8*   **$16.95**
"For days and days, nights and nights, I had dreamed of that first kiss which was to consecrate our engagement, and I knew not on what spot I should put my lips..."   Fiction/Classics Pages 240

The Art of Cross-Examination *by Francis L. Wellman*   ISBN: *1-59462-309-0*   **$26.95**
Written by a renowned trial lawyer, Wellman imparts his experience and uses case studies to explain how to use psychology to extract desired information through questioning.   How-to/Science/Reference Pages 408

Answered or Unanswered? *by Louisa Vaughan*   ISBN: *1-59462-248-5*   **$10.95**
Miracles of Faith in China   Religion Pages 112

The Edinburgh Lectures on Mental Science (1909) *by Thomas*   ISBN: *1-59462-008-3*   **$11.95**
This book contains the substance of a course of lectures recently given by the writer in the Queen Street Hail, Edinburgh. Its purpose is to indicate the Natural Principles governing the relation between Mental Action and Material Conditions...   New Age/Psychology Pages 148

Ayesha *by H. Rider Haggard*   ISBN: *1-59462-301-5*   **$24.95**
Verily and indeed it is the unexpected that happens! Probably if there was one person upon the earth from whom the Editor of this, and of a certain previous history, did not expect to hear again...   Classics Pages 380

Ayala's Angel *by Anthony Trollope*   ISBN: *1-59462-352-X*   **$29.95**
The two girls were both pretty, but Lucy who was twenty-one who supposed to be simple and comparatively unattractive, whereas Ayala was credited, as her Bombwhat romantic name might show, with poetic charm and a taste for romance. Ayala when her father died was nineteen...   Fiction Pages 484

The American Commonwealth *by James Bryce*   ISBN: *1-59462-286-8*   **$34.45**
An interpretation of American democratic political theory. It examines political mechanics and society from the perspective of Scotsman James Bryce   Politics Pages 572

Stories of the Pilgrims *by Margaret P. Pumphrey*   ISBN: *1-59462-116-0*   **$17.95**
This book explores pilgrims religious oppression in England as well as their escape to Holland and eventual crossing to America on the Mayflower, and their early days in New England...   History Pages 268

QTY

The Fasting Cure *by Sinclair Upton*   ISBN: *1-59462-222-1*   **$13.95**
*In the Cosmopolitan Magazine for May, 1910, and in the Contemporary Review (London) for April, 1910, I published an article dealing with my experi-
ences in fasting. I have written a great many magazine articles, but never one which attracted so much attention... New Age/Self Help/Health Pages 164*

Hebrew Astrology *by Sepharial*   ISBN: *1-59462-308-2*   **$13.45**
*In these days of advanced thinking it is a matter of common observation that we have left many of the old landmarks behind and that we are now pressing
forward to greater heights and to a wider horizon than that which represented the mind-content of our progenitors...   Astrology Pages 144*

Thought Vibration or The Law of Attraction in the Thought World   ISBN: *1-59462-127-6*   **$12.95**
by William Walker Atkinson   Psychology/Religion Pages 144

Optimism *by Helen Keller*   ISBN: *1-59462-108-X*   **$15.95**
*Helen Keller was blind, deaf, and mute since 19 months old, yet famously learned how to overcome these handicaps, communicate with the world, and
spread her lectures promoting optimism. An inspiring read for everyone...   Biographies/Inspirational Pages 84*

Sara Crewe *by Frances Burnett*   ISBN: *1-59462-360-0*   **$9.45**
*In the first place, Miss Minchin lived in London. Her home was a large, dull, tall one, in a large, dull square, where all the houses were alike, and all the
sparrows were alike, and where all the door-knockers made the same heavy sound...   Childrens/Classic Pages 88*

The Autobiography of Benjamin Franklin *by Benjamin Franklin*   ISBN: *1-59462-135-7*   **$24.95**
*The Autobiography of Benjamin Franklin has probably been more extensively read than any other American historical work, and no other book of its kind
has had such ups and downs of fortune. Franklin lived for many years in England, where he was agent...   Biographies/History Pages 332*

Name	
Email	
Telephone	
Address	
City, State ZIP	

☐ **Credit Card**   ☐ **Check / Money Order**

Credit Card Number	
Expiration Date	
Signature	

Please Mail to: Book Jungle
PO Box 2226
Champaign, IL 61825
or Fax to: 630-214-0564

ORDERING INFORMATION
web*: www.bookjungle.com*
email*: sales@bookjungle.com*
fax*: 630-214-0564*
mail*: Book Jungle PO Box 2226 Champaign, IL 61825*
or PayPal *to sales@bookjungle.com*

Please contact us for bulk discounts

DIRECT-ORDER TERMS

**20% Discount if You Order
Two or More Books**
Free Domestic Shipping!
Accepted: Master Card, Visa,
Discover, American Express